"I'd Be Uh...

The shock traveled through Kim's body, followed by a sharp jab of anger, which was compounded by the lascivious gleam in Jared's eyes and the unmistakable challenge in his face.

"You'd what?"

"I'd be willing to make arrangements for you to work off the debt this summer while you're not teaching."

"That type of ludicrous line might work on the many women who frequent your bedroom, but I'm most certainly not one of them!"

"Whoa! Hold on there. I don't know what you're assuming, but I'm offering a legitimate position, handling the summer office chores."

It made sense, but did she dare trust what he said? He was a Stevens. For as long as she could remember, their families had been enemies....

Dear Reader,

Revel in the month with a special day devoted to L-O-V-E by enjoying six passionate, powerful and provocative romances from Silhouette Desire.

Learn the secret of the Barone family's Valentine's Day curse, in *Sleeping Beauty's Billionaire* (#1489) by Caroline Cross, the second of twelve titles in the continuity series DYNASTIES: THE BARONES—the saga of an elite clan, caught in a web of danger, deceit…and desire.

In *Kiss Me, Cowboy!* (#1490) by Maureen Child, a delicious baker feeds the desire of a marriage-wary rancher. And passion flares when a detective and a socialite undertake a cross–country quest, in *That Blackhawk Bride* (#1491), the most recent installment of Barbara McCauley's popular SECRETS! miniseries.

A no-nonsense vet captures the attention of a royal bent on seduction, in *Charming the Prince* (#1492), the newest "fiery tale" by Laura Wright. In Meagan McKinney's latest MATCHED IN MONTANA title, *Plain Jane & the Hotshot* (#1493), a shy music teacher and a daredevil fireman make perfect harmony. And a California businessman finds himself longing for his girl Friday every day of the week, in *At the Tycoon's Command* (#1494) by Shawna Delacorte.

Celebrate Valentine's Day by reading all six of the steamy new love stories from Silhouette Desire this month.

Enjoy!

Joan Marlow Golan

Joan Marlow Golan
Senior Editor, Silhouette Desire

Please address questions and book requests to:
Silhouette Reader Service
U.S.: 3010 Walden Ave., P.O. Box 1325, Buffalo, NY 14269
Canadian: P.O. Box 609, Fort Erie, Ont. L2A 5X3

At the Tycoon's Command
SHAWNA DELACORTE

Published by Silhouette Books

America's Publisher of Contemporary Romance

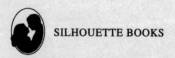

SILHOUETTE BOOKS

ISBN 0-373-76494-4

AT THE TYCOON'S COMMAND

Visit Silhouette at www.eHarlequin.com

Printed in U.S.A.

SHAWNA DELACORTE

has delayed her move to Washington State, staying in the Midwest in order to spend some additional time with family. She still travels as often as time permits, and is looking forward to visiting several new places during the upcoming year while continuing to devote herself to writing full-time. Shawna would appreciate hearing from her readers. She can be reached at 6505 E. Central, Box #300, Wichita, KS 67206-1924.

To Lola,

thank you for your valued friendship over the years.

One

"**S**he did what?" A shocked Jared Stevens swung his legs off the top of his large oak desk and jumped to his feet.

"She tore up the letter and threw it at me. Then, before slamming the door in my face, she told me, and I quote here, 'It will be a cold day in hell before I pay one penny to any member of the Stevens family.' She also said that any claim by you that her father owed a debt to Stevens Enterprises died when her father died." Grant Collins stood on the other side of the desk, a sheepish expression marring the attorney's otherwise dignified persona. "I've never had anyone do that before."

Jared's unmistakable anger surrounded his words, matching the irritation that shoved at him. "Just who does she think she is? I want you to—" He stopped and took a calming breath as he ran his hands through his thick dark hair. He narrowed his eyes and wrinkled his brow while turning a thought over in his mind.

"Never mind. I'll handle it myself." His tone of voice said the meeting was over.

As soon as his attorney left, Jared poured himself a cup of coffee and settled into the large leather chair. He picked up a file folder from the top of his desk, studied the contents for a few minutes while sipping his coffee, then leaned back and closed his eyes. He didn't have the time or patience for dealing with some old business transaction between his father and Paul Donaldson. The Stevens–Donaldson feud had been going on for three generations. He was tired of it and didn't care anymore what had started it or why it had escalated. He didn't have any interest in pursuing the matter with Paul Donaldson's daughter, either. He only wanted the past due twenty-thousand-dollar promissory note paid off so he could close out the matter. It was business, nothing personal.

He took a big swallow from his coffee cup. He had never met Kimbra Donaldson, but now it looked as if he would be doing battle with her whether he wanted to or not. The red numerals on his desk clock showed 4:30 p.m. The Donaldson house was only three miles from the Stevens family compound where Jared spent part of each summer since taking over the reins of Stevens Enterprises, even though he maintained a three-bedroom town house in San Francisco where he lived most of the year. The large estate doubled as his business office for a couple of months each summer when he retreated to his home town of Otter Crest on the northern California coast in an attempt to escape the congestion of San Francisco where Stevens Enterprises was headquartered.

He emitted an audible sigh. The matter of the promissory note had to be resolved as soon as possible so he could put it behind him and get on with real business. And that included the date he had that night with the stunning redhead he had met a week ago at a party thrown by a business associate in San Francisco. A little grin of expectation tugged at the corners of his mouth. It was almost an hour drive into the city, but it would be worth it for the night's pleasure he anticipated. But first he had to deal with the troublesome issue of Kimbra Donaldson. He placed the file folder in his attaché case, grabbed his car keys from his desktop and headed out the door.

Kimbra Donaldson had been in the same high school graduating class as his half brother, Terry Stevens. Terry's mother had been the second of what turned out to be a total of six wives plus numerous mistresses and short-term affairs for Ron Stevens. On many occasions Jared had thought how fortunate it was that his father didn't have more children by his many wives. When Jared left Otter Crest at the age of eighteen to go to college, Terry and Kimbra were ten-year-olds in elementary school. That had been twenty years ago.

Terry's opinion of Kimbra had not been very flattering, but Jared didn't put much stock in Terry's opinions. They hadn't been very close before their father's death five years ago, and Terry had been an ongoing problem for him ever since he had inherited the task of keeping an irresponsible Terry out of trouble.

Along with responsibility for Terry, he had also inherited the presidency of Stevens Enterprises. It had been a sobering dash of cold water thrown on his flamboyant social life, yet at the same time a stimulating challenge for someone who had been drifting through life without much purpose.

Jared drove down the street lined with older homes, checking the addresses until he found the house where Paul Donaldson had lived for almost forty years. He pulled into the driveway of the small house, turned off the engine and sat staring at the front door. An uneasiness settled in the pit of his stomach, and a strange feeling of apprehension welled inside him.

He had never dealt with any woman who had the gumption and assertiveness to rip up a demand for payment and throw it in an attorney's face. All the women he knew were decorative, fun-loving and always ready for a good time. And he had known plenty of them—women who were happy to embrace his philosophy of no strings attached and definitely no commitment.

He saw the curtain at the front window move a little bit. Someone was watching him. Jared took a calming breath. He couldn't put off the confrontation any longer. He needed to get the business resolved so he could be on his way to San Francisco and his female companion of the evening. He opened the car door, mindful that his every move was being scrutinized.

As he climbed out of the car, Kim Donaldson continued to watch him from behind the edge of the curtain. She had heard the car pull into the driveway but didn't recognize the silver Porsche. Then the door opened and the occupant climbed out. A hard lump formed in her throat followed by a sinking feeling of dread. Jared Stevens in person. She had allowed her anger to get away from her earlier and said a couple of things she shouldn't have. *Honestly, Kim, when are you ever going to learn to think before speaking and keep your big mouth shut?* She had no idea that her outburst with the attorney would produce such a quick, decisive and definitely unwanted response.

She swallowed the lump, took a deep breath and slowly exhaled. She had never met Jared Stevens, but she had seen him on a few occasions over the years when he had returned to Otter Crest during the summer. One such occasion had burned into her memory. She had been in high school. She had stopped to watch a softball game in the park and had immediately spotted one of the players dressed in cut-off jeans and a tank top. The physical attraction had been like a bolt of lightning.

Kim had fallen instantly in lust with the ruggedly hand-some young man in his early twenties without even know-ing who he was. The image had remained burned into her consciousness...the long legs, broad shoulders, strong arms and golden tan. Later she found out the man of her dreams was none other than Jared Stevens, Terry's older brother—the one the residents of Otter Crest always referred to as a womanizing playboy. She had immediately dismissed any interest in Jared Stevens. Their families had been feuding for generations, and there was no reason to assume he was any different than his brother, who she knew for a fact was an insufferable jerk, but the enticing image had remained with her all these years.

She watched as Jared leaned across the car seat and grabbed his attaché case. His jeans, T-shirt and running shoes belied his position as head of a multimillion-dollar corporation. A wave of anxiety swept through her. Should she pretend no one was home? No, that wouldn't serve any purpose. She had to face him if for no other reason than to reinforce her comments to his attorney. She had no inten-tion of paying him one penny of a debt her father had long claimed didn't exist. Besides, there was no way she could raise twenty thousand dollars even if she wanted to.

The ringing doorbell sent a nervous anxiety rippling through her body. She took another calming breath, but it didn't help. She opened the door to her uninvited visitor.

"Kimbra Donaldson?"

His voice sent little shivers through her. It sounded every bit as smooth and sexy as he looked. The years since that day when she had watched him playing softball had only enhanced his appeal. What were then youthful good looks had matured into incredibly handsome features combined with a magnetic appeal that reached out and grabbed her on the most primal level. And his eyes...she'd had no idea they were such an intense green. They were the type of eyes that could delve into the very core of a person's existence and uncover the innermost secrets hidden there. A sudden shortness of breath caught her by surprise. It was easy to see why so many women fell all over themselves in an attempt to get close to him. She shook away the unwanted thoughts and tried her best to rein in her rush of sensual excitement.

"Yes, I'm Kim Donaldson." *Calm down, breathe slowly.* Her self-directed instructions were wasted when she saw his gaze travel from her face down her body to her feet, then slowly climb her bare legs to her face again. There was no mistaking the lustful look that darted across his face, a look that said he liked what he saw. It was the type of look that made her feel naked and vulnerable while at the same time promising untold pleasures.

If only she had known he was headed her way she could have changed from the blue T-shirt and white tennis shorts she was wearing and would have stuck her bare feet into a pair of shoes. If she had been able to change clothes perhaps she wouldn't feel as if he was studying every curve of her body. A surprising jolt of excitement hit her—a sensation as disturbing as it was undeniably sensual.

"You prefer Kim rather than Kimbra?"

She nodded, words refusing to materialize.

"I'm Jared Stevens."

She finally found her voice but couldn't find a way of keeping her displeasure out of it. "I know who you are."

A flicker of surprise darted across his face, then quickly disappeared. "You were rather rude to my attorney this morning. In fact, Grant said it was the first time anyone had ripped up a letter and thrown it at him. I'm afraid your actions have forced me to take matters into my own hands." He stared at her for a long moment, then smiled...a devastatingly sexy smile that showed perfect white teeth in sharp contrast to the golden tan of his face. "I believe we have some pressing business to discuss."

A quick intake of breath was her immediate response to his smile, his nearness and the overwhelming power of his masculinity. It took all her inner resolve to maintain a semblance of composure while responding to his words. "We have nothing to discuss."

"We most certainly do, *Ms.* Donaldson." He made another obvious visual survey of her physical attributes before regaining eye contact with her. "We have lots to discuss."

The sparkle in his eyes intimidated her as much as it excited her. Her composure slipped away faster than she could keep hold of it. The last thing she wanted to do was appear in any way hesitant or unsure in front of Jared Stevens.

"May I come in?"

"Uh…" She tried to force some words, but nothing happened. She stepped aside and motioned him in, all the while berating herself for acting like some silly awestruck teenager. He was the enemy, not someone whose presence should render her tongue-tied.

She raked her fingers through her short blond hair, shoving it away from her face as she nervously cleared her throat. She gave it another try. This time the words managed to escape her throat in a businesslike manner.

"I don't see what we have to discuss. You're trying to extort money from me for a debt that doesn't exist. My father was very emphatic about that. I also think it's in very bad taste for you to swoop in like some type of vulture on the heels of his funeral to make your demands."

Jared cocked his head and raised an eyebrow. A quick look of surprise covered his features. "Extort? That's a rather harsh word to apply to an honest debt, one that's five years past due. If you were five years late in paying a twenty-thousand-dollar debt to anyone else, they would have had you in court by now.''

She fixed him with a hard stare and blurted out the first thing that came to her mind. ''If there was a legitimate debt, it would have been paid by now!''

He leveled a pointed look at her. Her blatant attempt at being as difficult as possible did not negate the obvious. Kim Donaldson was definitely a feast for the eyes, from the beautiful face to a body that would set any man's pulse racing—including his. His gaze wandered to the soft fabric of her T-shirt and the way it caressed the curve of her breasts, to her sleek tanned legs extending from her shorts and the russet polish on her toenails. He pegged her height at about five feet seven, a good match to his six-one. Her stubborn determination and the fiery glints of anger sparkling in her blue eyes did not dissuade him from entertaining the numerous erotic thoughts that had been circulating through his mind from the moment she'd opened the door. He forced his thoughts to the business at hand.

''I don't know where you got the impression that the debt isn't legitimate. Your father signed a promissory note with Stevens Enterprises for twenty thousand dollars, payable in full two years from the date of signing. In exchange for the promise to pay, your father received exclusive use of one of our warehouses for that two-year period of time. Having a promissory note rather than a lease agreement was your father's idea, an unusual request, which my father extended himself to accommodate. Shortly before the two years was up, my father died. Collection of the money due ended up in a state of limbo while the company changed from my father's hands to mine.''

He placed his attaché case on the coffee table, then withdrew a file folder. ''After taking over the company I was busy with several other matters, including restructuring part of the organization and developing new business areas.

Three years passed before the now severely overdue note was brought to my attention. For the past two years my corporate attorney and your father had been going around and around about the principal amount due plus all the accrued interest.''

Kim folded her arms defiantly across her chest in an attempt to put up a staunch front, but listening to Jared's description of the business transaction left her feeling a little uneasy and a lot uncertain. ''My father's account of the events differs quite a bit from your fanciful version.''

''My *version* is fact, and I have the appropriate documentation to back up my claim.'' Once again he flashed a devilishly disarming smile. ''If you have any proof of your father's side of this, I'll be happy to take it into consideration.''

Her anxiety level jumped up a notch or two. Jared was too self-assured, too smooth. She had never seen any paperwork relating to the matter. She only had her father's assertions. A shudder of apprehension swept through her consciousness. What if her father really did owe Stevens Enterprises twenty thousand dollars *plus* all the accumulated interest? She would never be able to pay that off. There hadn't been much money in her father's estate, and most of that went to pay for his funeral. As for his other assets, she would need to convert them to cash to pay what she considered his legitimate debts. Her savings amounted to only a little over two thousand dollars.

She gathered her determination. He was just trying to bluff her, to make her believe he had some kind of tangible proof. She was not going to fall for his line. It was the way the high and mighty Stevens family had been treating her family for three generations.

''If you have this proof, then I want to see it now.''

''Of course.'' His manner was almost condescending as

he smiled at her again, a smile that spoke volumes—a smile that said he had not been bluffing.

Jared opened the file folder and handed her copies of a signed contract and a signed, notarized promissory note for twenty thousand dollars. She fought to keep her hand from shaking as she stared at her father's signature. She carefully read both documents. It all looked legal and binding. A sinking feeling settled in the pit of her stomach. All her bravado crashed as the cold chill of reality sank in.

"I, uh, I want Gary Parker to look over these documents."

"Is that your attorney?"

"Yes."

"No problem." Jared stood, picked up his attaché case and walked to the front door. "I'll contact you in a couple of days to finalize the arrangements for the payment of the debt."

Kim watched from the window as Jared returned to his car and drove away. It had been a very unsettling meeting, caused as much by the way he made her senses tingle as by the stressful outcome of their conversation. Why had her father insisted the debt didn't exist when he had obviously signed a contract and a promissory note? She knew he couldn't have already paid out the twenty thousand dollars to settle the debt. As executrix of his estate, she had been over his finances.

A hint of despair settled inside her as her gaze drifted around the living room of the old house, the house where she had grown up, the house where she had lived until seven years ago—the house where just yesterday mourners had gathered following her father's funeral. Her father's sudden death at the age of fifty-five from a massive coronary had come as a shock to her. She had always thought of him as being in good health. He had never mentioned anything about heart problems, but her conversation with his doctor before the funeral told a different story. Her father had known of his heart condition but had chosen not to follow his doctor's orders.

She looked around the room again. It seemed like such a long time since she had moved from Otter Crest to accept her first job as an English teacher at a high school in San Francisco. In reality it had been only seven years, but it had been a very eventful seven years.

She had firmly established her career and earned the respect of her peers for her hard work and dedication to her teaching. She had twice been voted the most popular teacher by the student body of the school. The only downside had been her ill-fated engagement to Al Denton, a man whose idea of commitment to a relationship turned out to be that she was the one with the commitment and he was the one who could continue to date others.

Several months prior to the wedding, he'd changed. He had become overbearing, demanding, argumentative and controlling to the point where he made her life miserable. Whatever love she had felt for him quickly disappeared. She had broken the engagement, put the unfortunate experience behind her and gotten on with her life.

And now the past, in the form of Jared Stevens, had intruded into that neatly organized and smooth-running life.

She wandered into the kitchen and poured herself a glass of iced tea. How in the world could she ever pay off the debt, assuming it was legitimate? She didn't even know the exact amount. All those years worth of interest on twenty thousand dollars would make the debt even more insurmountable.

She returned to the living room and sank onto the corner of the couch. She took a sip of her iced tea, then set the glass on the end table. Her stress level had already been up due to her father's death, and now Jared Stevens had pushed it even higher. She leaned her head back and closed her eyes. A vivid image of Jared popped onto the screen of her mind—his handsome features, the sexy grin and the intensity of his eyes. She felt the overwhelming magnetic pull of his presence even though he was no longer there. Her heart beat a little faster, and her breathing quickened.

Kim's eyes snapped open, and she sat up straight. She didn't like the very disconcerting effect he had on her senses or the idea that there was something about him she found very appealing. Their families had been at odds for three generations. He was the last person on earth she should be having sensual thoughts about and definitely the last person she wanted or needed in her life.

Jared had spent an uneasy two days wrestling with his impression of Kim Donaldson. Thoughts of her had managed to intrude on the date he'd had following their meeting to the point where he had become distracted and couldn't concentrate on his stunning and willing companion of the evening.

Kim was not at all what he had anticipated and certainly not his type. After what his attorney told him about the meeting with her, he had fully expected to run into a disagreeable female hellcat. But much to his surprise, what he found was a beautiful and desirable woman who had instantly grabbed him in a way no other woman ever had. She set his pulse racing and definitely stirred his libidinous desires. But there was something else about her, something he couldn't identify. And it was that unknown quality that he felt sure was going to cause trouble of a kind having nothing to do with business.

He had given careful consideration to the fact that the debt might be beyond her means. If Paul Donaldson's house was any indication of his financial status at the time of his death, then Jared doubted that there was enough money in the estate to satisfy the debt plus several years of accrued interest. The small house was neat and clean, but the structure and its contents did not have much value on the open market. And being a schoolteacher meant Kim Donaldson was not in an income bracket that would allow her to easily assume a debt of that magnitude without having planned for the expense.

With a sigh of resignation and more than a little confusion about how to proceed, he gathered the appropriate paperwork and walked to his car. He had phoned and told her he would be there at 5:00 p.m. He knew he should have had her come to his summer office suite at the Stevens compound. That would have been more businesslike, more appropriate for the situation. But he hadn't suggested it. He chose to drive to her father's house even though it put the meeting on her home ground and on a more personal level. And he wasn't sure exactly why he had made that decision.

A low level of anxiety pushed at him as he drove to the Donaldson home. For the first time in his life he experienced a brief moment when he wanted to turn around and retreat from a problem. But that was not a practical solution to the issue. He toyed with the notion that it was Kim Donaldson who had caused his apprehension rather than the circumstances of the business matter. The possibility made him nervous, something very unusual for the always-confident Jared Stevens.

As he climbed the steps to the porch, Kim opened the door. On more than one occasion over the past couple of days he had visualized the beautiful barefooted woman in the shorts and T-shirt—her slightly mussed hair giving her an earthy look, her full lips revealing a sensuous mouth, a flash of emotion sparkling in her blue eyes even though that emotion had been anger.

A little pang of disappointment jabbed at him when he saw the conservative way she had chosen to dress for their appointment. Unlike the first time he had arrived at her father's house, she wore a simple white blouse, charcoal gray slacks and low-heeled shoes. His realization of that disappointment said more than he wanted to know. In their one brief meeting she had managed to capture his undivided attention and hold on to it. She was as much of a puzzle as she was a fascinating woman, far more complex than the women he usually associated with.

Kim stepped aside as he entered the house. At that moment he regretted his decision to set the appointment away from his office. This was one business meeting that he wanted to have over as quickly as possible. A little shiver darted up his spine. He had a strange sensation of upheaval, almost like a premonition that his life was about to take a strange detour from his intended course.

He sat on the couch, making a concerted effort to appear casual. He wasn't as sure about how to proceed as he had been two days ago when he'd confronted Kim Donaldson. He gathered his determination. The debt wasn't a personal matter, it was a company financial transaction and as such needed to be resolved.

"Has your attorney looked over the documents?"

Kim nervously shifted her weight from one foot to the other, then finally sat down in a chair on the opposite side of the coffee table. For the previous hour she had been rehearsing what she wanted to say when he arrived, but now that he sat across from her, that confidence started to erode. He looked so calm and in control, as if he didn't have a worry in the world, while in contrast her stomach churned in knots.

"I met with him yesterday."

"And?"

She forced out the words, her voice barely above a whisper. "He tells me it's a legal, binding agreement." She glanced at the floor, unable to meet his steady gaze. It had been the most difficult thing she had ever said, far more so than when she'd told her fiancé the engagement was off and they were through.

"Then I assume you're prepared to pay the debt."

Kim squared her shoulders, steeled her determination and forced herself to make eye contact with him. A quick ripple of anxiety darted across her skin. "No...I won't be paying the debt. This apparent obligation was my father's business transaction, not mine. You have no legal claim against me or anything I own."

"You think not?"

A nervous tickle poked at her consciousness as she watched him place the document in his case. He closed the lid and snapped the locks shut. He stood, picked up the attaché case, then turned toward her—every movement, every gesture, slow and deliberate, sending a wave of trepidation through her body.

He cocked his head and shot a curious look in her direction. "Not paying the debt...is that the advice of your attorney?"

"I didn't consult him beyond his inspection of the documents. It's simply the way it is."

"You realize that you're leaving me with no choice other than to file a claim against your father's estate, which will tie it up for quite a while and prevent you from selling or otherwise disposing of any of his property, such as this house and its contents."

Kim's breath caught in her throat, and a hard knot twisted in the pit of her stomach. Had she heard him correctly? Everything about Jared looked very determined. Her legs trembled to the point where she feared they would no longer support her as the seriousness of what he said sank in. How would she ever be able to fight a multimillion-dollar corporation on a matter that her attorney said was a legal obligation? The anxiety churned through her body as a throbbing headache attacked her temples.

She needed the money the sale of her father's house would bring to pay off his debts. She couldn't afford to have his estate tied up in court. A wave of anger threatened to erupt. Jared was nothing more than a predator circling his prey. He had chosen a time when she was most vulnerable and had pounced on the opportunity. He had taken unfair advantage of a situation just like the Stevens family had been doing to the Donaldsons for the past three generations.

She tried to rally her courage while forcing a calm to her anger. "Then I'll consult my attorney about that."

"I have legal counsel on staff. You'll have to hire an attorney, and it will probably end up costing you more than simply paying the debt your father owes."

At that moment his tone reminded her exactly of her ex-fiancé's overbearing and controlling manner. She fought the urge to lash out at him for trying to manipulate her life and causing all this trouble. Then a realization hit her. Which *him* was she talking about? Was it her ex-fiancé or Jared Stevens who had earned her recrimination? She pulled her composure together and tried to look at the situation in a logical and dispassionate manner. He was only trying to collect a debt he believed was owed by her father. She tried to convince herself that it didn't have anything to do with the Stevens–Donaldson feud. He wasn't trying to control her life or go out of his way to make trouble for her. It was a straightforward business arrangement, nothing more.

And the enormity of that business nearly overwhelmed her—the amount of money at stake and Gary Parker's words that it was a legal binding contract and the promissory note was, indeed, long past due. He had told her that Stevens Enterprises had every right to exercise their legal muscle in collecting it. A sinking feeling settled inside her, effectively shoving down whatever fight she had left. She was in a very precarious situation. Being defiant wasn't going to help matters. She needed to find some sort of cooperative middle ground with Jared Stevens in order to resolve the money situation without putting everything in jeopardy.

Her voice quavered, her words barely above a whisper as despair filled her. "I can't afford to pay the debt. There's no way I can raise that kind of money. I need the proceeds from the estate to pay several other obligations of my father's."

The strong determination had vanished, and in its place Jared saw a vulnerable woman who didn't seem to know what to do. He had been prepared for Kim's strong stance. He could handle her anger. He knew he was more than capable of dealing with any business negotiation. But this touched him on a surprisingly personal level, and he wasn't at all sure how to handle it.

He allowed his gaze to drift over her features. A tightness pulled across his chest. Yes, indeed—she was an incredibly desirable woman who had definitely heated up his libido.

He turned on the charm that never failed to produce the desired results, but the words were out of his mouth before he could evaluate where they had come from—words that were as much lustful desire as they were serious.

"Perhaps we could reach a compromise. According to my attorney, you're a high school teacher. I'd be willing to let you, uh…" His words trailed off as his libido shoved at him again. He flashed a smile that was as much pure seduction as it was sincere. "To work off the debt."

Two

The shock traveled through Kim's body, followed by a sharp jab of anger, which was compounded by the lascivious gleam in Jared's eyes and the unmistakable challenge in his face.

"You'd what?" A hard edge surrounded her words, combined with her disbelief at what he had said, but she didn't care and made no effort to hide it.

"I'd be willing to make arrangements for you to work off the debt this summer while you're not teaching rather than having to come up with the money from some other source."

A hint of a grin tugged at the corners of his mouth, a grin he was obviously trying to suppress. Anger welled inside her. He was playing games with her, baiting her...taunting her. She bristled at his suggestion and its implied meaning, a situation fueled by the sexy twinkle in his eyes. She forced her anger down as she carefully measured her words. "That type of ludicrous line might work on the many women who frequent your bedroom, but I'm most certainly not one of them!"

"Whoa! Hold on there. I don't know what you're assuming, but what I'm offering is a legitimate way for you to resolve this problem. I need a girl Friday type of person for the summer while I'm here. I usually have one of the secretaries from our corporate offices in San Francisco handle the summer chores, but I'd be willing to allow you to fill that position. And in exchange for that..." His voice trailed off as his gaze slowly drifted across her body, then returned to her face.

The anger crept into her voice. "And in exchange for that, what? You're going to forgive twenty thousand dollars plus all the accrued interest?" She threw a skeptical look in his direction. "That's a lot of money for only three months worth of *legitimate* work."

He stared at her. She felt as if his green eyes were looking right through her. A shiver of trepidation slowly replaced the anger of a moment earlier. Had she gone too far? Had she been out of line in so quickly jumping to interpret his meaning or, more accurately, to possibly have misinterpreted it? She couldn't afford to be on the receiving end of a lawsuit. She could not allow the situation to disintegrate to the point where he would file a claim against her father's estate. *Good grief, Kim. Why can't you learn to keep your big mouth shut and your thoughts to yourself?*

"It would be a lot of money if it were actually being paid to someone. I'm looking at the overall picture, the cost to me of bringing someone from the corporate offices. Not only would I need to pay someone a salary while taking them away from their regular duties, I would also need to provide housing for the summer and per diem money since that employee would be away from home on a work assignment. You already have housing here in Otter Crest, and I assume have already made arrangements for whatever money you need to accommodate your bills during the summer."

It made sense, but did she dare trust what he said? He was a Stevens. For as long as she could remember, her father and Jared's father had been at odds. And before that it was her grandfather and Jared's grandfather. The walls seemed to be closing in around her, trapping her in an untenable situation. He had manipulated her to the point where he had taken away any choices she might have had.

She tried to project an assertive, in-control attitude, something far removed from the way she felt. "I would insist that my attorney draw up a document stating the exact parameters of this agreement…that is, *if* I decide to do it."

Jared flashed the sexy smile that set her heart fluttering and caused a shortness of breath. "I wouldn't have it any other way—everything neat and tidy and legal."

She swallowed hard as several thoughts circulated through her mind. It didn't have to be all one-sided where she was doing all the giving and he was doing all the taking. There wouldn't be anything in an agreement that said she had to be pleasant. She could make it the most miserable three months of his life as long as she didn't step over the line and give him an opportunity to claim she wasn't living up to her part of the agreement. But was that practical? What she really wanted to do was resolve the debt question, then get as far away from the town of Otter Crest and any connection with the Stevens family as she could.

A brief thought popped into her mind that it might be the sexy magnetism of the troublesome and disconcerting Jared Stevens she wanted to get away from. She tried to dismiss the errant notion as ridiculous, but it continued to linger in the back of her mind, circulating a heated excitement through her veins.

Jared's smooth voice interrupted her disturbing thoughts. "Well? What's your answer?" The triumphant gleam sparkled in his eyes, and the look of victory covered his features. "Are we going to be able to satisfy this debt easily or do I need to have my attorney file that claim against the estate?"

A hard lump formed in her throat, successfully blocking any attempt to speak. He had her backed into a corner. A little shiver of trepidation worked its way through her body, touched by a hint of resentment at the way he had manipulated the situation for his benefit. She reluctantly nodded in agreement. Would it be a decision she would live to regret? One that would come back to haunt her?

"Is that nod your way of accepting my offer?"

She forced the words. "Yes…providing my attorney can draw up an agreement that we both find acceptable."

Jared opened his attaché case again and removed a writing pad and pen. He seated himself on the couch. "Now, what points do you want to have in the agreement?"

It was another half hour before Jared prepared to leave the Donaldson house. They each had a list of the points they had agreed to. He had offered to have his attorney draw up the letter of agreement, but she had insisted she wanted her attorney to do it. The agreement would take effect on Monday. That would give him four days to devise a work schedule for her and to figure out exactly what he would be having her do.

A little twinge of delight danced inside him as he walked to his car. She could have her attorney draw up the agreement, but as long as it followed the parameters they had agreed to he would be able to give her a whole list of menial tasks and mundane little chores.

Jared climbed into his car, backed out of her driveway, then drove down the street. He had many legitimate projects where he could use the help of a good assistant during the course of the summer, not the least of which was the community center building currently under construction, but could he really trust her to handle confidential business matters for him? To work with his best interests in mind? He wished he could, but he was afraid to take that chance. She had already made it clear the Stevens–Donaldson feud was prominent in her thinking. So he would confine her work to unimportant jobs that did not compromise his business interests or jeopardize any important projects.

He continued to turn the possibilities over in his mind as he drove home. Once again a sense of upheaval in his life burrowed its way into his consciousness, leaving him a little bit uneasy and very uncertain about what the next three months would bring.

Kim stared at the clothes she had brought with her from her apartment in San Francisco. She tried to determine what would be appropriate to wear her first day of work at Jared's summer office. She glanced at the clock next to the bed—6:30 a.m. A touch of irritation shoved at her, just as it had for the past few days. She had two hours of freedom left, then her contracted work schedule would deprive her of her summer.

She had spent the last three days clearing out some of her father's belongings—donating his clothes to a homeless shelter, examining his financial records in more detail, then contacting his creditors about his financial obligations. She determined what she wanted to keep and what she would sell, obtained an appraisal of his belongings and listed his house with a real estate agent. The only things she had not inspected were several file folders containing miscellaneous papers. The pressing business matters of her father's estate had been attended to for the time being. She placed the file folders in a box and set it aside. She would look at the papers some other time.

Her attorney, Gary Parker, had presented her with the letter of agreement according to the points she and Jared had previously established. They had both signed it. And now there was nothing left to do except show up at Jared's summer office at the Stevens family compound. A jitter of anxiety confirmed that she was far from comfortable about what she had agreed to. She slowly shook her head. It was too late to back out, especially with the huge debt looming over her.

She finally chose a casual outfit of slacks, a simple pullover and sandals. She tried to eat some breakfast, but a nervous energy insisted on twisting her stomach into knots. She settled for some coffee, orange juice and an English muffin, then drove the short distance to the Stevens family compound and Jared's office.

Kim pulled up to the curb across the street from the large estate. She sat in her car staring at the massive two-story house. A compendium of thoughts and emotions swirled inside her, leaving a very uneasy sensation in its wake. This was the land that Jared's grandfather, Victor Stevens, had cheated her grandfather, George Donaldson, out of in a dishonest poker game. It was the single incident that had set her grandfather against Jared's grandfather, which had started the Stevens–Donaldson feud. An intense wave of trepidation left her unsettled.

Kim had never been on the property, never passed through the upright bars of the iron gate that led to the large house behind the high brick wall. The one-hundred-acre land parcel, which fronted the ocean, had been the single most prized possession of her grandfather and the central core of his financial worth. The loss of the land broke him both financially and in spirit. He had made so many plans for the land, plans he knew would end up bringing him a fortune. Instead, Victor Stevens used the ill-gotten land to elevate the already significant Stevens family fortune to new heights.

All her life she had heard about the land swindle and how Victor Stevens had ruined her grandfather, how his son, Ron Stevens, had carried on the Stevens family tradition of trying to cheat the Donaldsons. She never understood why her father had continued to do business with Ron Stevens. Her mother had been noncommittal about it, but her father refused to let the subject drop. Kim had lived with all the anger and resentment her father carried around with him, all the stress his attitudes brought into the house. She had been relieved to escape the tension when she went to college and finally moved to San Francisco when she procured her teaching job.

She stared through the open gates at the large house. The estate covered a mere two acres of the original one-hundred-acre property but had its own private beach and boat dock. The rest of the land had been sold to developers for several million dollars, money that should have been in her family, not the already wealthy Stevens family. And now she was in the uncomfortable position of working for Jared Stevens, helping him propel Stevens Enterprises toward even greater financial success.

She set her jaw in determination. She needed to honor the terms of the letter of agreement and satisfy her father's financial obligation to Stevens Enterprises, but there was nothing that said she needed to be pleasant or amiable around Jared. She put her car in gear, drove through the gate and up the long driveway.

The closer she got to the imposing structure, the more

her confidence drained away until it had been replaced by rampaging anxiety. By the time she had parked in front of the large double door, she needed to force herself out of the car. She took a steadying breath and climbed the three steps to the porch. Her hand trembled slightly as she reached for the doorbell.

A moment later the door swung open and a man in his late fifties dressed in bib overalls and an old plaid shirt, greeted her. "You Miz Donaldson?"

"Yes."

He stood aside and motioned her in. "I'm Fred Kemper, the estate caretaker. Jared's expectin' you." He started down a long hallway indicating that she should follow him.

She glanced through the archway from the entry foyer into a large, tastefully and expensively decorated living room with a cathedral ceiling, a loft that ran around three sides and a large fireplace. Beyond that was a formal dining room with a crystal chandelier. She quickly counted the chairs around the table—twenty of them. She had never seen a dining table of that size in a private home.

Everything spoke of wealth, elegance and prestige. A jolt of resentment swept through her, followed by a wave of anger. This should have belonged to her family. It should have been her grandfather's and then her father's. It would have given her mother an easier life, making the few years she'd had much more comfortable, and would probably have allowed her father to live longer than his fifty-five years. But it had not been so. Victor Stevens had taken that option away from her family when he swindled her grandfather out of the land.

"This way."

Fred's voice jerked her out of her thoughts. She followed him down the hallway that ran along the inside of the front wall of the house, then through a door into what was obviously a much newer area than the rest of the house. Suddenly she found herself standing in the middle of an office complex.

"Jared will be right along in a minute."

Kim watched as Fred headed back the way they had come. As soon as he was out of sight she seated herself on a couch, then took a minute to inspect the office. Everything she saw seemed efficient and streamlined, modern, with all the latest equipment enabling Jared to conduct major business from his house.

His house. She clenched her jaw to ward off the anger that once again threatened to override her attempt at maintaining a calm demeanor. She had never given the land or the Stevens family compound much thought until Jared's attorney had approached her about the promissory note. Until that moment she had considered the entire land swindle history, something that had a serious impact on her father's life but did not involve her. Now she found herself reluctantly thrown into the middle of the generations-old feud.

And it all felt very personal.

Her gaze made another sweep of the office area. It was the opinion of most of the people in town that Jared was nothing more than a playboy squandering the fortune he had inherited, that he was merely a figurehead providing a family member as president of the corporation. The real work was undoubtedly done by qualified people who were dedicated to their jobs. So why had he gone to all the trouble and expense of constructing an office wing, and what kind of work could he possibly have for her to do?

A frisson of apprehension darted through her body, an uneasy feeling telling her she might have made a bad bargain for herself in accepting his offer to work off the debt. She closed her eyes, and a mental image of Jared immediately popped into her mind. Once again the intensity of his green eyes and his devilishly sexy smile assailed her senses. A little tremor of excitement told her Jared Stevens was the cause of her apprehension, not the Stevens–Donaldson feud, as she wanted to believe.

"I'm glad to see you're on time."

Jared's smooth voice sliced through her wandering thoughts and startled her to attention. Her eyes snapped open. The sight that greeted her did nothing to dampen her aroused senses or stop her errant musings. He stood framed in the doorway of what appeared to be an inner office beyond the reception area. A shortness of breath caught her by surprise. He might not be the handsomest man in the world, but at that moment she couldn't imagine who would win out over him. With his head cocked to one side, his arms folded across his chest and his hip leaning against the door jamb, he looked like someone she wanted to get to know much better.

She took a steadying breath, then shoved the disturbing thoughts from her mind. True, she hadn't been dating anyone lately and had no special person in her life, but Jared Stevens was the last man she needed to be having desirous thoughts about. His family was responsible for the ruination of her grandfather and the bitterness that had controlled her father's life for as long as she could remember. Jared Stevens was the enemy. She could never let herself forget that.

"I try to always be punctual, Mr. Stevens." She wanted to kick herself. The words sounded far too strained and definitely way too nervous. That was not the impression she wanted to convey, not the way she wanted to start the first day. She squared her shoulders and stood up. She had to project confidence, an image that said he may have coerced her into this ridiculous situation but he was not going to control her.

He leveled a sharp look at her, briefly making eye contact. "Call me Jared. Mr. Stevens was my father." He chose to ignore her tone of voice and her blatantly obvious attempt to be disagreeable. If that was the game she wanted to play, she would find that she had more than met her match.

He straightened, slowly crossed the room and perched on the edge of the desk without taking his eyes off her. He had hoped she would have somehow changed since he had seen her so her presence wouldn't continue to pull at his senses, but no such luck. His pulse jumped and raced as he forced his breathing under control. She was every bit as beautiful as he had pictured her over the past few days, every bit as desirable as he feared she would be and definitely a huge temptation. He took a steadying breath. He had a busy workday ahead of him and needed to keep his mind on business. He didn't have time for personal thoughts of lust—at least, not at the moment.

He rose from the edge of the desk as he gestured toward the coffeepot sitting on the credenza against the wall. "Grab yourself a cup of coffee if you want, then I'll give you a quick tour of the office complex before we start work." Kim poured herself a cup of coffee as Jared waited.

"This—" he walked over and opened a door that went to the outside "—is the entrance to this wing of the house and is used for the business offices. It's the door you'll use from now on rather than the front door to the house. As you can see, there's a driveway from the side street that goes past the garage and there are parking spaces right here by the door." He handed her a key card. "This will open the side gate." She stuck her head out the doorway and took a quick look around. He closed the door and headed in the direction he had come from a few minutes earlier, explaining as he walked.

"This room is the reception area where my summer assistant works. This—'' he waved his arm as he stepped into a smaller room containing a table and six chairs ''—is used as a conference room.'' He continued through another door into the innermost room of the office wing with Kim right behind him.

''This is my office.'' He reached across the desk, grabbed some papers and quickly shoved them into a file folder. Until—or maybe that would be *if*—such time as he could trust her with the details of his business dealings he wanted to keep certain papers away from her observation.

Kim surveyed her surroundings. It was a large office with a double set of French doors leading out to a patio, allowing him to come and go without anyone in the conference room or reception area seeing him. She stepped through the French doors. A chain link fence separated a large yard from the rest of the property. A doghouse just off the patio said it was a place where a pet could have lots of outdoor space without interfering with the rest of the property. About twenty feet away were windows that looked into a kitchen and another door into the house.

On the other side of the fence along the back of the house was a large deck next to a swimming pool and a hot tub. Beyond that the property sloped down to the beach and was enclosed by the same type of tall brick wall that surrounded the front of the property. A flower-lined path wound leisurely through the yard and past several trees to a gate leading to a private dock. Moored at the end of the dock was a gleaming white sailboat with bright blue canvas covers over the furled sails. Everything spoke of money and prestige, of a life filled with ease and comfort.

And it had all been stolen from her grandfather by Jared's grandfather. It should have been in her family.

''This is very nice, certainly quite luxurious.''

''Thank you. I only wish I could spend more time here

rather than at my town house in San Francisco, but that's where the company offices are and where I need to be most of the time.''

She clenched her jaw to keep her negative thoughts from turning into words as she returned to his office. She spotted the file folder on his desk. His furtive attempt to hide the papers had not escaped her notice. Were the papers something personal or business? A little wave of disgust rippled through her. It was probably another of the many shady business deals the Stevens family had been involved in over the years. She tried to muster her determination. One thing was for sure—there was no way she would be party to any of his underhanded dealings. If he thought—

''Do you get along with animals?''

His words grabbed her attention. She had been so absorbed in her thoughts she hadn't realized he had been talking to her.

''Uh…animals?''

''Yes. That's the first item on the list of things for you to do today.'' He handed the list to her. ''I don't expect you to use your own car to haul Lurch to the groomer. You can use one of my vehicles. The Ford Explorer is the one Lurch is the most comfortable in.''

''Lurch? The groomer?'' She wrinkled her brow as she stared at the list without focusing on any of the words. A shrill whistle penetrated her confusion. She looked up just in time to see Jared whistle again, then a large dog with a huge head entered through the open French door and came loping across the office directly toward her. Her first thought was to get out of the huge animal's way, but she couldn't move fast enough. She stared, helpless, as the massive animal bore down on her.

Everything happened so quickly Kim wasn't sure of the exact sequence. The animal stood on its hind legs with its paws on her shoulders. Whether the dog knocked her down or she stumbled and fell, she wasn't sure. A second later she found herself sprawled on the floor with an energetic Saint Bernard licking her face. She frantically tried to shove the animal away from her, but the more she squirmed the more the dog seemed to think it was a game.

Jared grabbed the dog's collar and gave it a gentle tug. The unmistakable sound of amusement surrounded his words. "Come on, Lurch. Let Kim up." He let go of the dog, who gave Kim one more slurp against her cheek, then retreated to the other side of the room.

Jared reached his hand out to help Kim. She hesitated, then accepted his assistance. The moment their hands touched an unmistakable surge of sensuality traveled up her arm and infused itself through her body. He easily pulled her from the floor as if she weighed no more than a feather. She tried to remove her hand from his all-too-tempting touch, but he refused to let go. Instead, he pulled her closer to him until their bodies were almost touching. She looked into his face, and once again the intensity of his green eyes delved into the very core of her existence.

Jared continued to hold on to Kim's hand. As much as he wanted to kiss that delicious-looking mouth was as much as he knew he didn't dare make the attempt. His words came out much softer than he had anticipated. Even though he wanted to maintain an impersonal atmosphere, he was finding it difficult.

"Are you all right? Lurch didn't hurt you, did he?"

She eased her hand out of his grasp, leaving him with a sudden and unexpected sense of loss. He didn't know what disturbed him more, the loss of physical contact or the desire to have it back.

Kim tried to dismiss the unwelcome surge of desire that swept through her when he pulled her body close to his.

For a moment she thought he might try to kiss her, a situation that, to her surprise, wasn't an unpleasant notion. She tried to brush aside the unacceptable thoughts and cover her errant desires by adjusting her rumpled clothing. She attempted to wipe her face with her hands.

"What in the world was—"

"That was Lurch. Sometimes he gets a little rambunctious. He doesn't usually take to strangers, but he seems to like you."

She looked at Jared as a combination of disbelief and outrage welled inside her. "That's Lurch? You expect me to take that huge beast to the groomer?"

"Watch what you say." He feigned a worried expression. "Lurch is very sensitive."

She shot him an angry glare, then stooped and picked up the list the dog had knocked from her hand and began to read. "Take Lurch to groomer. Pick up dry cleaning. Have Porsche detailed."

The moment of desire that had assailed her senses quickly disappeared to be replaced by suspicion and irritation. She narrowed her eyes as she stared at him. "This is your idea of the type of work you expect from me? I thought you wanted a secretary for the summer, someone to do office work, not someone to run mundane errands for you and do menial little tasks."

He adopted an attitude that was all business. "I don't believe there's anything in our agreement that specifically limits your duties to secretarial work."

"But I assumed—"

Jared shoved a set of keys into her hand. "Lurch will never be comfortable in that little thing you drive. Take the Explorer. It's parked just outside the door."

"Wait a minute!" She bristled at what she saw as his

take-charge attitude and controlling nature. "We need to talk—"

"You'd better hurry. They're expecting Lurch at nine o'clock." With that, Jared turned and went into his office, leaving Kim standing in the reception room staring at his retreating form. It had never occurred to her to have the letter of agreement specify that her work assignments would be confined to office chores. She clenched her jaw in anger. He had planned this entire scenario just to embarrass her. This is what he had in mind all along. The situation would definitely require a conversation with her attorney about this unexpected turn of events.

She looked at the keys he had given her and glanced at the list again. On the back he had written the name and address of the dog groomer, the dry cleaner and the car detailer. She turned toward the dog, who was sitting next to the desk. Lurch looked at her with big brown eyes, his tail wagging and his muscles tensed as if it was all he could do to sit there quietly.

Some of the stress that had wrapped itself around her stomach started to loosen a bit. Now that she had gotten over the shock of the large Saint Bernard charging toward her, she had to admit to herself that he was a magnificent dog. "Well, Lurch, it looks like we're going to the groomer. Do you have a leash or something?"

The dog cocked his head and stared at her for a moment, then trotted toward Jared's office, his powerful wagging tail knocking over a wastepaper basket as he went. She looked at what were now her wrinkled and dirty clothes. If this was the way it was going to be, then jeans and a T-shirt would certainly be appropriate dress for the rest of the summer. It was apparent she wouldn't need to be concerned about maintaining an image in front of Jared's clients or business associates or to be presentable for a business office.

A strange sensation washed over her. Half of it was resentment that he had purposely deceived her about her duties and relegated her to such an insignificant position, but the other half was relief. Even though she had been curious about the business holdings of Stevens Enterprises, she really didn't want to be involved in any of Jared's business dealings.

She tried to look at it in a logical manner. The thing for her to do was to make the best of a bad situation. Perhaps it was nothing more than a game of one-upmanship, his way of making sure she knew he was in charge. Maybe it was better this way. She would let him think he had the upper hand. If her summer job at Jared's involved nothing more than running errands, then that's the way it would be. It would certainly be an easy way to satisfy her father's debt and resolve the entire problem without involving an attorney or any more legal ramifications. It was a situation she knew she could live with for the three-month duration of the letter of agreement.

Lurch came running into the room with one end of a leash in his mouth and the other end dragging on the floor behind him. The dog sat in front on her, dropped the leash, barked and wagged his tail. He acted more like a playful puppy than a huge animal sitting in front of her anxiously waiting to go somewhere. She picked up the leash and attached it to the dog's collar. The dog immediately took off toward the door, pulling Kim behind him.

"Whoa! Slow down, Lurch." She couldn't stop the laugh that spontaneously erupted in reaction to the dog's excitement at going somewhere. It took all her strength to control the animal and keep him from dragging her across the floor.

The sound of her laughter carried to Jared's office. He stood in the doorway watching Kim trying to contain the dog as it hurdled through the door into the parking area and toward the green Explorer.

He liked the sound of her laugh but could not see her face. He wondered what her smile looked like. He had been face-to-face with her three times, and on all three occasions not even a hint of a smile had crossed her otherwise beautiful face. He closed his eyes and pulled up the still-fresh memory of her hand in his as he helped her from the floor, of the sensation of her face close enough to his to have leaned over and kissed her delicious-looking mouth. A tightness pulled across his chest, one that told him just how much Kim Donaldson had intruded into his conscious thoughts and desires.

And he didn't like it…at least he *thought* he didn't like it.

Business or pleasure—each confrontation made him less sure of his intentions where she was concerned. Something told him he should have written off Paul Donaldson's promissory note as a bad debt and closed the books on it. If only he had listened to that something instead of opening his mouth and letting that foolish plan of her working off the debt become reality. He had wanted to ruffle some Donaldson feathers. It had been an incredibly stupid idea, but it was too late now.

He attempted to calm his nerves. She was intelligent and could definitely be a big help to him during the summer, but could he trust her? Would he ever be able to trust a Donaldson enough to share Stevens Enterprises business matters? Would there ever be an end to the ridiculous Stevens–Donaldson family feud? One thing was for sure. He would have to keep her busy and away from his office if he planned on being able to concentrate on business. It was already more than evident that she was far too distracting to have around.

He forced himself to work but could not wipe the vision of Kim Donaldson from his mind, nor could he erase the sensation of her hand in his. A hint of trepidation told him the days ahead would be anything but normal. And the notion of exactly what that meant caused another twinge of anxiety to assail his senses.

Kim Donaldson spelled trouble with a capital ''T'' and he had no one to blame but himself.

Three

Kim could not settle the nervous jitter that appeared the moment she slid behind the wheel of Jared's silver Porsche. It was the same nervousness she experienced earlier when she had driven the expensive sports car to the detailers. It was a beautiful car, sleek and powerful, just like its owner, she reluctantly admitted. She had been surprised when he had handed her the keys with no more fanfare than to ask her if she knew how to drive a manual transmission.

If she owned a car like that there was no way she would ever let anyone else drive it, certainly not someone who might have a motive to damage it. Although she wouldn't do such a thing. What if it accidentally got scratched or dented? Would he think she had done it on purpose just to spite him? She didn't know what to think anymore. During the course of the day she had entertained one thought after another about what type of man Jared Stevens really was.

She came up with a different answer each time. He had clouded her thoughts from the moment she met him.

She glanced at her watch as she put the car in gear. It was almost five o'clock. All she had to do was return Jared's car to him, then she could call it a day. All in all, it hadn't been such a bad day. She had made friends with Lurch, who was definitely just a big, overgrown puppy in spite of the fact that he was three years old.

But the big, overgrown puppy's owner was a different story. Every time she returned to the office complex, every time she was in the same room with Jared, the electrical energy that filled the air almost overwhelmed her, leaving her with very unsettled thoughts and feelings. It was as if she could reach out and actually touch his sexual magnetism.

He had given her a few office tasks to do—routine letters about one of the corporation's holdings taking out an ad in a trade periodical, employee participation in a civic fundraiser, a couple of requests from charitable organizations and some memos to department heads, but it was obvious that he had kept her away from anything someone could use to compromise his business concerns. It was apparent he didn't trust her, but she had to admit she understood why. If their roles were reversed, she certainly wouldn't trust him with any confidential business matters.

Most of the office chores were related to personal business rather than company functions. He had given her a list of phone calls to make, changing the day of the week for the pool service to clean the swimming pool, making arrangements for a newly purchased billiard table to be delivered, having the liquor store deliver several cases of wine and scheduling a time for the carpeting to be cleaned. They were all chores she thought Fred Kemper, the estate caretaker, would have handled.

Even when she had her back to Jared she could feel him watching her. It left her uncomfortable and excited all at the same time. What kind of a man was Jared Stevens? So far, in spite of the fact that he had misled her about the nature of the work she would be doing, he didn't seem to be the same type of jerk as his brother.

Terry Stevens had been cruel with his cutting comments and put-downs. He had lorded his family position over everyone, especially Kim. He had done his best to belittle and humiliate her, and she had never forgiven him for it. Jared, on the other hand, had pretty much left her alone all day, other than to outline what he wanted her to do. She did have to reluctantly admit that every time she had been at the office during the day he had been at his desk and looked busy. It had not been as bad as she'd anticipated.

She drove Jared's Porsche through the service entrance gate and parked it in the garage, then entered the office complex through the direct outside door. She walked through the reception area into the conference room, then paused at the door of Jared's office. He was leaning back in his large leather chair with his feet propped on his desk, but he looked far from relaxed. His total attention seemed to be riveted on the document he held. From her vantage point, it appeared to be a contract of some sort. With his knitted brow and an unhappy scowl covering his face, he looked angry about something.

She hesitated, not sure if she should interrupt him. Maybe she could just deposit his car keys on the desk in the outer office and leave without him knowing she was there, but she waited too long. As she was about to turn, he looked up and saw her.

"You brought my car back?" He swung his legs off his desk, rose to his feet and started across the office toward her.

"Yes." She held his keys out toward him. "I guess I'll be going home now."

"Not so fast, Kim." Their fingers brushed slightly as he took the keys from her hand, causing a ripple of excitement to dart across her skin. "We're not quite finished for the day."

She glanced at her watch. "It's almost five-thirty. I've been here since a little after eight o'clock this morning. What is there that can't wait until tomorrow morning?" A hint of irritation pushed at her. "Is there some other menial little task that you feel should be pushed off on me? Do I need to run out and fetch the newspaper for you? Check the mailbox and bring in the mail? Take the dog for a walk? Rearrange the kitchen pantry so that all the food is in alphabetical order?" She leveled a challenging stare at him. "Well? What is it?"

He captured her look and held it with his unwavering gaze. Her irritation quickly turned to embarrassment. Once again his eyes seemed to be reading her innermost thoughts and feelings. And her thoughts at that moment were certainly less than complimentary toward Jared Stevens, but they were also enveloped in a sensually elevated heartbeat.

His silence made her embarrassment grow until she was forced to break eye contact with him. She attempted to maintain her position and determination, but her confidence crumbled. She tried to swallow the lump in her throat. "Well…" She nervously glanced around the office in a desperate attempt to avoid eye contact. "What is it that I still need to do tonight before I can leave?"

"Fred brought in the mail, I already have a newspaper, the food in the pantry is just where it needs to be and Lurch has a big hunk of two acres in which to run and exercise."

She bristled at his condescending tone, partly because she knew she deserved it. Perhaps she had gone too far with her inappropriate comments. Even though she had originally planned to make the situation uncomfortable for him, she had not been able to go through with the ill-conceived plan. It was not her nature to initiate confrontation in spite of the fact that there was something about him that seemed to bring out the worst in her. Every time he opened his mouth she became defensive.

She waited, hoping he would say something else, something to help relieve the awkward discomfort rapidly building inside her. Something to let her know she hadn't been that far out of line with her flippant gibes.

It seemed as if an eternity passed before he spoke again, an eternity that left her stomach twisted in knots. Why did he have to be so sexy, so desirable? If only she could dismiss him from her mind as easily as she did with her words.

His voice gave her no indication as to what was going on inside him, how her harsh words had affected his decision. "What I had in mind was checking the refrigerator to see what's there and fixing something to eat. I thought maybe I could put a couple of steaks on the grill and you could make a salad." He cocked his head and shot her a questioning look. "Unless you have other plans for dinner?"

Had she heard him correctly? Dinner? That's what he had in mind? Now it was more than simple embarrassment that filled her. It had been a long time since she felt this foolish. Once again the magnetic sex appeal of Jared Stevens worked its way into her reality. Would they be alone in the house or would Fred be having dinner with them? What were Jared's motives? Could she trust him on a personal level? Perhaps the better question would be could she trust herself alone in a social setting with this very appealing man—a man whose family had been feuding with hers for three generations.

She hesitated, not sure exactly how to respond to his unexpected invitation. "I, uh, no, I don't have any other plans. I suppose having something to eat would be okay." Now what? She had agreed to his request. A nervous twinge told her it might be a decision she would soon regret.

"Good. Let's go raid the refrigerator. I'll bring up a bottle of wine from the wine cellar and while I'm doing that you can feed Lurch." He headed down the hall, indicating that she should follow.

She stood there, dumbfounded. He had done it to her again—dangled something reasonable in front of her and then as soon as she had agreed to it he quickly added a menial task. It was the same as when he allowed her to work off the debt thinking she would be doing office work. Then he had her run mindless personal errands for him. She shoved down the anger that tried to take hold. She didn't want to lose her temper with him and blurt something that would only make things worse—again—but she did want to make her position very clear.

She clenched her jaw in determination and tried to put a calm tone to her voice without being wholly successful. "Feed the dog? That's some technique you have there...dangle some nice courtesy in front of me, then hit me with your real intention. Well, it's not going to work this time. Now that I think about it, I do have a previous engagement. So, if you'll excuse—"

The doorbell rang, followed by someone pounding loudly on the front door, then the door flew open with a bang. A tall man with dark hair burst into the entryway. He glanced around as if looking for something. His harried gaze fell on Jared. "I need a favor."

Kim immediately recognized the new arrival as Terry

Stevens, the Stevens family member who had tormented her all through her middle school and high school years.

Jared's tightly controlled words surprised her. They showed a combination of practiced restraint and exasperation. "You always need a favor. What is it this time?"

Terry carefully eyed Kim as if he had just noticed her standing there. He turned toward Jared. Sarcasm dripped from his words. "What's she doing here? Is this 'be kind to a Donaldson week'?"

A quick flash of anger darted through Jared's eyes. "What she's doing here is none of your business."

Terry turned to her as he gestured toward the front door. "Run along, Kim. Jared and I have a personal matter to discuss."

Jared immediately stepped between Kim and Terry, cutting off anything she might have said in response to Terry's bad manners. "Kim and I were about to have dinner. Since you are not invited to join us, it appears that you're the one who needs to *run along*."

Kim tried to collect her thoughts. She was rattled and confused. Jared had definitely usurped her position in speaking for her, but had he also just taken her side and defended her against the verbal barb from his own brother? Had he told Terry that he was not welcome and he should leave right away? She had been angry with Jared just moments before Terry's unannounced arrival. Now she didn't know what to think.

Terry shot an angry sidelong glance at Kim, then turned his back on her and lowered his voice, but not so low she couldn't hear what he was saying. "We have some personal business to discuss and it can't wait until you've fed Kim."

"Yes, it can wait. Business can wait until business hours. I have some free time at ten o'clock tomorrow morning. You can stop by the office then."

Terry's demanding and aggressive attitude softened a little. "But you don't understand what the problem—"

Jared's voice turned hard and his manner abrupt. "I understand fully well what the problem is. I was just going over the contract that Tony Williams was kind enough to messenger to me this afternoon. The contract promising payment in thirty days. The contract you had no authority to sign. The contract that obligates Stevens Enterprises to pay a hundred thousand dollars for something the company will never see because it will immediately become another one of your toys. Does that convey a proper understanding of *the problem?*"

Terry nervously glanced at Kim again, then pulled Jared aside. "This is a matter that should be discussed in private, certainly not in front of a Donaldson."

"As I told you, ten o'clock tomorrow morning." Jared turned away from Terry, then glanced at him. "And be on time. I have a very busy schedule tomorrow."

Jared took Kim's arm and escorted her from the foyer into the main part of the house, leaving Terry standing in the entryway. She wasn't sure exactly what to say to Jared but knew she needed to say something. "Uh...back there when you told your brother—"

He cut off her words before she could say anything else. The bitterness in his voice was unmistakable. "Terry is my *half* brother, not my brother. Terry is the result of daddy dearest's second marriage...or perhaps it was his third marriage. I tend to lose track of the total number of women who have been Mrs. Ron Stevens."

He furrowed his brow in mock concentration for a moment. "No...it was his second wife. I think he had a total of six wives...of course, there could have been one or more wives prior to my mother that I'm not aware of. And that doesn't count the mistresses in between and sometimes during the numerous marriages.''

Jared's manner quickly changed to a pleasant, upbeat attitude. ''Now, before we were so rudely interrupted I believe you were trying to convince me—'' the loud slamming of the front door announced Terry's departure, but Jared didn't stop walking or look toward the door ''—that you have another engagement for this evening. I'm going to assume you meant for later this evening, something you needed to do after we have dinner.''

She managed some barely audible words in response to Jared's take-charge manner. ''I suppose so.'' She offered no resistance as he steered her through the house to the large gourmet kitchen. He had done it to her again, coerced her into something she had no intention of doing. Why did she end up caving in and letting Jared have his way? What happened to her determination to stand up to him? Why did her resolve seem to go into hiding whenever she was around him?

Jared continued through the kitchen into the large utility room. He opened a door that led downstairs. ''I'll be right back with a bottle of wine.'' A hint of a mischievous grin tugged at the corners of his mouth. ''Lurch's food is in the cupboard, and his food and water dishes are on the floor over there in the corner.'' He disappeared down the stairs before she could say anything.

Kim stood motionless as she thought about her options. Just when she was prepared to do battle with him over her dog-feeding assignment he had done an about-face in his attitude and stepped in front of her, blocking Terry's verbal attack...both figuratively and literally. She was still a little flustered about Jared's confrontation with Terry and confused by the way he seemed to have protected her. There was also the sharp edge to his voice when he made it clear to her that Terry was his half brother. It was the last thing she ever would have anticipated, especially from a member of the Stevens family.

A warm feeling settled inside her as she replayed his words in her mind. He hadn't embarrassed her by saying she was working off her father's debt, he had simply told Terry that her presence was none of his business.

Uncertainty darted through her. Jared Stevens had a very disconcerting affect on her, one that left her apprehensive about his motives and at the same time excited every time he came near her. Just the sound of his voice sent excitement coursing through her. She stared at the door where he had disappeared as she tried to figure out what to do.

She could ignore what he had said about feeding the dog, but to do that seemed rather petty. A three-generations-old family feud was certainly not the dog's fault. She emitted a little sigh of resignation. She would try to sort it out after she got home. But for now… She opened the cupboard he had indicated, took out the bag of dry food and set it on the counter. When she stooped to pick up the dog bowls she caught sight of something so ludicrous it took her completely by surprise.

There, in the middle of the back door, was the largest doggy door she had ever seen. It was big enough for a good-size man to crawl through, allowing any stranger access to the house. The absurdity of it tickled her to the point where she couldn't restrain her laughter.

Jared reached the top of the stairs, bottle of wine in hand, as her laughter reached his ears. The sound surprised him and at the same time captivated his senses. It was the same laugh he had heard earlier that day but had not witnessed— a disarming laugh that sent little ripples of excitement through him. A moment later he saw that her smile was equally enchanting. A tightness pulled across his chest, and his pulse raced a little quicker, the same physical reaction that assailed his senses every time he was close to her.

He wasn't sure why he had insisted she stay and have dinner with him. It was the same type of impetuous decision that had led him to make her the offer of working off her father's debt. Something about her made him want to keep her close. Was it a mistake? Would he eventually regret it? Probably, but that was an intellectual concern, and he seemed to be acting on pure emotion, first his libido and then something he couldn't identify, something that told him he liked having her around and wanted to get to know her better.

He entered the utility room. "What's so funny?"

She spun around, her eyes momentarily wide with surprise and her cheeks showing the crimson blush of embarrassment. "You startled me. I didn't hear you come back."

He offered her a sincere smile, one that held neither deceit nor subterfuge. "With all that laughter going on I think a truck could have rattled through here without you hearing it."

"It's, uh..." She suppressed another giggle as she gestured toward the dog door. "It doesn't matter what kind of a security system you have for your house, that dog door is large enough for any burglar to fit through."

He chuckled as he shook his head in amusement. "Well...I sort of assumed that anyone thinking about breaking in would decide an animal requiring that big an entrance was one they wouldn't want to encounter."

She offered a shy smile. "I suppose that makes sense."

"Besides—" in an involuntary action he reached out with his free hand and lightly touched her cheek and hair "—the security system covers the other doors from the utility room to the kitchen and the one leading downstairs...."

His voice trailed off as he set the bottle of wine on the counter next to the bag of dog food. He knew he was treading on dangerous ground, but at that moment he didn't care. He also knew he had no business instigating anything of a personal nature with her, especially under the circumstances, but his desires overpowered the thin thread of common sense that still clung to him.

He ran his fingers across her cheek and down her arm, then grasped her hand in his. The words slipped out on their own without him consciously wanting to say them. "You have a very nice smile. You should smile more often."

Still clutching her hand in his, he pulled her body closer in much the same way as when he had helped her up from the floor that morning. Only this time he didn't stop. He leaned forward, brushed his lips against hers, then captured her mouth with a soft kiss. He tasted the earthiness of a sensuality that nearly knocked his socks off. He felt her hesitate for a moment as if she was uncertain what to do, then she turned her face away and broke off the kiss.

Her voice contained a combination of shock, embarrassment and anger. "What do you think you're doing?"

He didn't move away, his face still within inches of hers. "I was indulging an impulse."

Kim glanced nervously around the utility room. Her body was sandwiched between Jared and the counter so she couldn't back away from him. In spite of the excitement coursing through her body, she tried to sound authoritative, in control and businesslike.

"You may feel free to indulge your impulses with the many women you date, but I'm not one of them. This is strictly a business arrangement, and I'd appreciate it if in the future you would refrain—"

Lurch charged through the dog door, slid across the

smooth tile floor and bumped into Jared, knocking him off balance. Jared fell against Kim. In an awkward moment, each instinctively grabbed for the other in an attempt to remain upright and regain their balance, but they ended up in a tangle of arms and legs on the utility room floor with his body partially covering hers. Jared's face was again very close to Kim's. He made no effort to release her or stand up.

"Are you all right?" He didn't like the huskiness that surrounded his words, a verbal indication of what was going on inside him and much more than he wanted to reveal. He wanted to kiss her again, to experience her taste. His desires told him he would be happy to spend the evening right there on the floor with her, their bodies pressed together. His logic, however, told him it was a bad idea, a situation he should put a stop to immediately regardless of how much she stimulated his passions.

He skimmed his fingertips across her cheek and tucked an errant lock of hair behind her ear. "Lurch didn't hurt you, did he?"

"I'm...no, he didn't hurt me." A sensual wave swept through her. She felt the rise and fall of his chest as his body pressed against hers, matching her increasingly labored breathing. Her skin tingled where his fingers touched it. Everything about this was as wrong as it could be. It was bad enough when he had tried to kiss her and she had almost allowed it. Now they were on the floor with his body on top of hers, and neither of them was making any effort to put a stop to it.

She should have refused his dinner invitation. She should have slapped his face when he tried to kiss her. She should be pushing him away from her so she could get up. So why hadn't she done any of those things? It was a question she didn't want to think about. The conclusion could say more than she wanted to know.

Kim forced herself to take action. She pushed against Jared, marveling at his hard muscled shoulders and at the same time wanting to break the physical contact. "Let me up."

Jared reluctantly got to his feet. As soon as he stood, Lurch started licking Kim's face. He grabbed the dog's collar. "Lurch...shame on you." He sent the dog across the room, then reached out his hand to Kim. It was probably just as well the moment was brought to a halt, but he couldn't stop the thoughts about where things might have gone if Lurch hadn't come charging into the room.

"This is the second time today I've had to help you up from the floor." He fought the wry smile that tugged at the corners of his mouth. "You're going to have to learn to keep your feet under you."

Kim ignored his offer of assistance and scrambled to her feet. The kiss had her far more rattled than being knocked to the floor in another encounter with Lurch. And what had her even more unnerved was the knowledge that she wanted to be a willing participant in that kiss. She quickly ran her fingers through her mussed hair as she tried to regain her composure.

She put forth a businesslike attitude, desperate to move away from the very personal and intimate moment they had just shared. "Yes, and both times it was because your dog knocked me down."

Jared glanced toward Lurch, then returned his attention to Kim. His voice teased and his eyes sparkled with humor. "As I said this morning...I think he likes you."

She tried to ignore Jared and pretend the previous few minutes had not existed. In the hope of covering her embarrassment and stilling the excitement that continued to ripple through her, she grabbed the bag of dog food from the counter and poured some into Lurch's dish. Next, she took the nearly empty water dish to the utility sink and filled it. And all the while she felt his gaze on her, which only compounded the desire surging through her body— unwanted desire. *What in the world will the next three months be like if I'm having this much difficulty getting through the first day?* It was a question that left her very uneasy.

After placing the water bowl next to the dog's food dish, Kim took a deep breath, held it a moment, then slowly expelled it in an attempt to steady her shaken nerves. She turned toward Jared. A quick jolt of anger, combined with a hint of embarrassment, shot through her consciousness. He looked so calm and composed, as if kissing her had been nothing more than business as usual and hadn't meant anything to him beyond saying hello.

Her anger and embarrassment merged into a feeling of resentment at the way he had tried to use her and guilt over the way she had allowed the kiss to happen. She wasn't sure what to say to him, or what to do.

The one thing Kim was sure about was her need to get out of his house and away from the mesmerizing sex appeal of Jared Stevens. She adopted a formal, businesslike attitude as she straightened her clothes. "I've fed the dog. I assume that concludes my chores for the day."

He seemed genuinely surprised by her statement. "But what about dinner?"

"I have a previous commitment." With that, Kim turned and walked away from Jared.

Jared started after her. "Wait a minute—" He caught up with her in the entryway by the front door. "What commitment?"

She clenched her jaw in anger. "My personal life is none

of your business. The only thing that's your business is our agreement for me to work off my father's debt, and I'm beginning to regret having said yes to it." Her voice dropped to a whisper. "There must be some other way to handle the financial obligation."

He flashed a knowing smile, one that said he had the upper hand. "Yes...I'm sure there is."

He brought his mouth down on hers again. It was a kiss that started soft but quickly escalated. Once again he sensed her hesitation, but a moment later, much to his surprise and pleasure, she returned his kiss.

This wasn't what he had anticipated, wasn't what he had in mind when he suggested they have dinner. At least he didn't think it was what he had in mind. But as soon as she responded positively all his thoughts stopped...all except the one that told him he was in real trouble. Whatever was going on inside him, whatever it was that had pushed him to do something he knew he shouldn't was more than physical desire and lust. He chose to ignore the disturbing thoughts about what it could be.

Kim knew she should not be kissing him, should not be standing there giving him her cooperation rather than her indignation. There was no doubt in her mind she would live to regret her actions, but it was something she was going to have to worry about at some other time. Right now his kiss was all she wanted to know about. She thought she had experienced toe-tingling kisses before, but they were nothing compared to the sensuality of Jared Stevens. She would deal with self-recriminations and guilt later.

She started to slip her arms around his neck but caught herself in time. His embrace tightened, sending a tremor of anxiety through her body. This was wrong, very wrong. She had to break it off immediately and make sure he understood that under no circumstances would it happen again.

She summoned all the self-control she could muster and finally managed to step away from him while fighting to bring her breathing under control. The heated flush of excitement spread across her cheeks. Her embarrassment prevented her from looking at him. She reached for the door, then quickly ran out of the house.

''Wait!'' Jared's voice reached her but she refused to respond to his shout. All she wanted was to get away from the intoxication of his mesmerizing presence.

Four

Jared stood at the door and watched as Kim's car moved down the long driveway. Confusion and mixed feelings swirled around inside him. He wanted to go after her but knew it would be a mistake, just as his actions had been a mistake. It was the first day of their work agreement. He had expected a lot more objection from her about the tasks he had given her, but to his surprise she hadn't made too many protests.

Things had gone smoothly…right up until he had insisted she stay and have dinner with him. Even Terry's interruption had not put a damper on what he had hoped would be a pleasant evening. He wanted to know his adversary a little better, not as man and woman, not as opposite sides of a feud, but rather as one person to another. He wanted to know about her understanding of the generations-old family feud. What was her side of the numerous incidents over the years that had fueled the conflict? Why did she think their families had continued to do business together in spite of the hard feelings raging around them?

The only things he really knew about the Donaldsons were his father's ongoing battles with Paul Donaldson and Terry's comments about Kim. The opinions of his half brother and his father were not important to him.

He closed and locked the front door of the house, retreated to the kitchen, opened the bottle of wine he had brought from the cellar, then popped a frozen dinner into the microwave. He stared at the large Saint Bernard who sat next to him as if waiting for something to happen.

"Well, Lurch, what do you think of Kim? I think she likes you. She must—" he chuckled softly at the memory of Lurch knocking her to the floor on their first meeting "—otherwise she probably would have told me to *get that damn dog* off her." He bent on one knee and lovingly stroked the dog's head and scratched behind its ears. "So, what do you say? Do you think the two of you can be friends? That means you have to stop knocking her to the floor."

Lurch cocked his head as if considering Jared's words, then let out a loud bark and wagged his tail.

Jared stood. "I'll take that as a yes." He poured himself a glass of wine, stared at the microwave and watched the timer count down the seconds until his dinner was done. As soon as it was ready, he took his meal from the oven and carried it and his glass of wine to the den. It would be another evening spent at home in front of the television.

A quiet laugh, half amusement and half irony, escaped his throat. It was not exactly the high-living lifestyle of a womanizing playboy. He allowed a little scowl to wrinkle across his forehead. Tomorrow was a very busy day, and he had to add Terry's latest fiasco to his workload. He clenched his jaw in anger. This time his irresponsible half brother was not going to get away with using the corporate offices to secure his personal toys. If Terry wanted a new sailboat, he could find the money to pay for it himself.

Jared's thoughts turned to Kim, to the heated moment when she had briefly responded to his kiss. It certainly hadn't been his common sense that had been in charge when he'd kissed her. Not only had it been a totally inappropriate action, considering the circumstances, it had been just plain stupid on his part. He couldn't deny the attraction but was unable to understand it.

Perhaps it had been a bad idea to coerce her into working off her father's debt. A twinge of guilt poked at him—especially in light of his subsequent suspicions about the validity of that debt. Paul Donaldson had signed a promissory note and a contract. It was legitimate, but there was still something about the transaction that didn't sit right with him. Knowing his father's penchant for underhanded dealings, and with the feud raging between the two men, the more he thought about it the more he believed there was something wrong with the deal. He didn't have any evidence, but the possibility disturbed him.

What would happen if Kim discovered irregularities among her father's papers? Would she think he had a hand in it? It was too late to terminate the letter of agreement and consider the matter closed. She would understandably want to know why he had suddenly changed his mind after being so insistent about payment. Leave the deal intact or terminate it? It seemed that either way could produce unwanted results.

Troublesome and conflicting thoughts continued to circulate through his mind for the rest of the evening, occupying his attention until he finally went to bed.

Kim spent a very unsettled evening and a restless night. Sleep had been intermittent, and she finally got out of bed at five-thirty. Work began at eight-thirty. She stared at herself in the bathroom mirror. She hoped she could cover the dark circles under her eyes with some makeup.

Confusion ran rampant as she thought back to the previous evening at Jared's house. How could she have allowed him to kiss her like that? And worse yet, she had gone so far as to respond to that kiss and had come within a fraction of a second of putting her arms around his neck. It was so unlike her. She was not into casual relationships, indulging an impulse, as Jared had said. She was not impulsive, either.

An unexpected chuckle caught her by surprise when she recalled the way she had torn up the letter and thrown it at Jared's lawyer. Perhaps she was occasionally impulsive, but not in her personal relationships with men. She had learned that lesson when she had impulsively become engaged to what turned out to be the wrong man.

So what if Jared's kiss curled her toes and took her breath away? There was no denying it was a good kiss. *A good kiss. Who do you think you're kidding? It was a great kiss.* A quick surge of irritation set a frown across her forehead. *He's had a lot of practice. He should have it down to perfection by now.* But that didn't excuse her actions or ease her guilt. *Honestly, Kim, how did you get yourself in this mess? And how are you going to get yourself out of it?*

As much as Jared excited her, the idea of continued contact with him over the summer frightened her. Where it could lead scared her even more. Several times during the night she had allowed a fleeting thought of what it would be like to have Jared make love to her, a thought that embarrassed her and disturbed her.

She had turned the problem over in her mind for most

of the night and had not come up with anything that resembled an acceptable plan of action. Everything came back to that letter of agreement she had foolishly insisted on, the one that said she would work for Jared to satisfy her father's debt. If she refused to show up for work he could file that lawsuit against her father's estate, and she couldn't afford to have that happen. She felt truly trapped between what she had to do and her fears about where her attraction to Jared Stevens could lead.

She checked the time, grabbed a quick shower, forced down some breakfast and dressed for work. Promptly at eight-thirty she drove onto the grounds of the estate and entered the office complex.

To her surprise, Jared was at his desk with papers and file folders spread across the surface. She watched him for a few minutes. He seemed totally absorbed in work and not aware of her arrival. She thought of the previous day. Each time she had been in the office he seemed to be hard at work. Maybe she had been a little hasty in her assumption that he was nothing more than a figurehead who left all the work to others. The memos he had her type showed decisions coming from him rather than him asking for other people's advice about what to do. Of course, they didn't involve any serious business decisions, but still...

The ringing phone interrupted her thoughts. She turned toward the desk in the reception area, intending to answer it, but Jared grabbed it before she could get there.

"Stevens." After a brief pause, Jared's voice turned angry. "I'm not going to discuss this with you on the phone. We have an appointment for ten o'clock. We'll discuss it then." He slammed down the receiver, then sat staring at the phone for several long moments before shoving back from the desk. He grabbed the carafe from his credenza and poured coffee into his empty cup, but only a couple of swallows came out. Obvious irritation covered his face as he turned toward the open French doors in his office.

"Fred, are you out there?"

Fred Kemper stepped into the office from the patio, a watering can in his hand. "You need somethin'?"

"Are you busy? I seem to be out of coffee. Could you…"

Fred emitted a soft chuckle. "Sure. I'll fix up a new pot." He cocked his head, glanced at his watch and stared at Jared for a moment. "It ain't even nine o'clock yet and you've already gone through that much coffee? You must have a passel of problems on your mind this mornin'."

"I do. In addition to the labor situation at the Oakland plant, contract negotiations on the purchase of a small fabricating shop, a collection problem with a client who looks like he's on the verge of bankruptcy and some shoddy merchandise from a new vendor we were trying out, I have one of our biggest clients pushing me to host some kind of a fund-raiser for his wife's favorite charity."

"Don't you have other folks who are supposed to be takin' care of some of that for you?"

A sheepish grin caught the corners of Jared's mouth. "Yeah, I do…but sometimes I have trouble divorcing myself from the day-to-day and delegating to the proper department heads. It's something I really need to work on. Maybe I should just take off one of these days and go sailing…clear out my head and totally relax."

Jared heaved an audible sigh. "And as if all that isn't enough, I have to confront Terry in a little over an hour about his latest caper."

Kim saw a hint of fatigue on Jared's face as he recited the list of problems he'd been wrestling with. As much as she hated to admit it, she felt a rising admiration for his management abilities and his willingness to accept responsibility.

Jared handed the empty carafe to Fred, then turned toward his desk. Kim saw a look of surprise dart across his face when he spotted her standing in the doorway.

He offered a tentative smile. "I didn't hear you come in. Have you been standing there long?"

"No, I just arrived."

Jared motioned toward the open French door. "Fred will have some coffee here soon." He glanced at the nearly empty cup in his hand, then looked at her with a guilty grin. "Apparently I drank the entire pot I made a couple of hours ago."

Kim glanced at her watch. "It's only eight forty-five. How long have you been at your desk?"

"Since about six-thirty. I have a lot of things to do today and needed to get an early start."

Jared had not made any mention of what happened between them the previous night. Had that type of behavior been so routine for him that he didn't give it a second thought? Kim wasn't sure what to say or how to act. An involuntary reaction to the memory of his kiss caused her fingers to go to her lips. She could still feel the heat of his passion, which only went to inflame the memory. Tension churned in the pit of her stomach.

She nervously ran her fingers through her hair and shifted her weight from one foot to the other. "Well, if you'll give me my list of chores for the day—" she inwardly cringed when she heard the negative edge she had put on the word *chores,* something she hadn't intended to do even though she still felt a certain level of resentment about the menial tasks. "Uh, I mean if you'll tell me what you want me to do, then I can get out of your way so you can go back to work."

Jared immediately caught her uneasiness and the edge in her voice. He had been so busy all morning he hadn't had time to think about the previous evening...or perhaps it was that he didn't want to think about it. He had managed to do away with the awkward feeling until he turned and saw her framed in the doorway.

Myriad emotions, thoughts and feelings circulated through his consciousness. He regretted making the advances toward her, but at the same time he was not sorry he had kissed her. Her taste, the sensation of having her in his embrace...they had left an indelible impression on him. And he didn't know what to do about it.

"Uh, sure." He turned toward his desk and picked up a list he had made first thing that morning. The tension shoved down on him. Perhaps not mentioning the incident would be the best way to proceed. He held out the list to her.

She took it from him and glanced over the items. "Well, another day of mostly menial tasks and errands." The words had escaped without her meaning them to. She regretted having said them but could not deny her displeasure. She caught the quick look of amusement that darted across his face—as if he was taunting her with lowly errands. Was that his game? His purpose in having her work? She glared at him, which he seemed not to notice.

Jared gestured toward the list. "First thing is a trip to the vet for Lurch. It's time for his annual rabies shot and new tags—"

As if on cue, when his name was mentioned, Lurch came charging in through the French door and headed straight for Kim.

This time she was prepared. She braced herself against the desk and waited for the inevitable, but it didn't happen. Instead of jumping up and putting his paws on her shoulders, Lurch settled his body next to her and leaned his one hundred eighty pounds against her leg while he enthusiastically wagged his tail.

Kim reached down and stroked the dog's head. It was a relief to have the tension broken. "Come on, Lurch. I guess we're off to the vet's office."

She took the dog for his shots and an hour later returned to the office complex with Lurch. She turned the Saint Bernard loose in the backyard using the gate at the side of the garage, then went around the building and entered the reception area rather than cutting through Jared's office. She poured herself a cup of coffee, settled in behind the desk, then looked at the next item on her list. She was halfway through typing a memo when a familiar voice cut into her concentration and interrupted her work.

"What did Jared do—" an unmistakable note of condescension surrounded the words "—hire you to work for him? Is this his donation to charity?"

She glanced up and saw Terry Stevens standing in front of her desk. A smug look of superiority covered his features. Anger rippled through her body. The years since high school had not changed him at all. He had been an arrogant jerk then, he had been rude last night, and this morning his attitude was equally untenable.

Jared's voice intruded. "Your appointment is with me, not Kim." He turned and walked into his office. Terry shot one last disdainful look at Kim, then followed Jared.

Kim rose from her chair and edged her way closer to the small conference room that separated the reception area from Jared's office. She felt a pang of guilt—eavesdropping wasn't polite—but her curiosity got the better of her sense of right and wrong. The ensuing argument between the two men was loud enough that Kim could easily hear what was said in spite of the fact that Jared had closed his office door.

"I've had it with you, Terry, and with your totally ir-responsible attitude about everything. This hundred-thousand-dollar contract you signed for the sailboat is null and void. I've made it clear to Tony Williams that you have no authority to sign contracts in the company's name, and if he sells the sailboat to you, the corporation will not be financially liable for the payment. That it's between him and you, and if—"

Terry's angry response cut off Jared's words. "You have no right to do that!"

"Wrong!" Jared's anger matched Terry's. "I have every right to make that decision."

"Apparently that decision only applies to me. I notice that you still have your sailboat docked out back."

"That sailboat was paid for by me personally, not with corporate funds. As president and chairman of the board of Stevens Enterprises, I'm responsible for seeing that the cor-poration is run in an ethical manner while making a profit and that's not been easy with some of the shady deals Dad pulled off.

"As for you...for some reason you seem to feel that you're entitled to whatever you want without having to work for anything. Dad left you with a monthly income large enough to cover your living expenses. It's up to me to determine if that allowance needs to be increased. You're not a kid anymore. You're thirty years old. Until you can show some responsibility and initiative, there won't be any more free handouts coming from the corporation. If what you have isn't sufficient, you might try getting yourself a job...although I can't imagine what you'd be qualified to do."

The voices dropped, preventing Kim from hearing what was being said. She returned to the reception desk and con-tinued with her work, although Jared's words about the importance of ethics and his having problems with some of his father's business deals circulated through her mind. A few minutes later Jared's office door banged open, and Terry stormed through the reception room and out to the parking area.

"I want to apologize for Terry."

Kim turned toward Jared. His words caused a flash of surprise to dart through her. Jared Stevens apologizing to her? This was certainly unexpected.

"He never learned good manners. His mother instilled a *you are better than everyone else and are entitled to whatever you want* type of attitude in him predicated on the family money, and he's yet to figure out that it just isn't so."

She covered her embarrassment. "That's all right. I got used to his rudeness in high school."

"It's not all right." Jared extended a sincere smile. "But it's nice of you to say so."

He captured her gaze and held it. The air sizzled with the sexual energy between them. He tentatively reached out and touched her cheek, then quickly withdrew his hand. He didn't want to take a chance on things getting out of hand as they had the previous night. He didn't want to do something he knew he had no business doing. What was there about Kim Donaldson that made him want to throw out all the rules and shove his common sense aside? The question left him uneasy, but not as uneasy as he feared the answer would.

At that moment he truly regretted suggesting she work off her father's debt. Then an equally disturbing thought flashed through his mind. Could his decision to let the letter of agreement stand be due to his desire to keep Kim Donaldson close to him? A hint of panic told him how awkward and uncomfortable he found that possibility. It was not like he lacked feminine companionship, even though his dating habits had been greatly curtailed since he took over as president of Stevens Enterprises.

"I, uh..." He nervously shifted his weight from one foot to the other. "Well, I was wondering if..."

He didn't like the hesitancy in his voice or the feeling of not being sure of his words or actions. He took a calming breath and regained his composure. "I have lots of work to do, and you have your list. We both have enough to keep us busy for the rest of the day."

Jared quickly returned to his office. He had almost asked her if she would help him plan the charity fund-raiser for his client. It was something he had been thinking about that morning. It would mean they would be working together on a project. It would entail long hours spent in each other's company and would assure them working together past the specified term in the letter of agreement. It certainly held the possibility of developing an intimate closeness...but it also held the possibility of disaster.

He walked through the open French door to the patio. It was a beautiful day—sunny, bright and warm. The type of day to be spent outside enjoying what nature had to offer. Terry's sailboat fiasco had started him thinking. It had been quite a while since he'd been out on the water. He allowed his mind to drift to the days when he had lots of free time to indulge his passions, one of which was sailing.

Jared had been surprised when he took over the company. Until that time, underhanded dealings and unethical decisions on his father's part had only been vague suspicions. He had been able to convince himself they had nothing to do with him. But the moment he took over they became reality. He knew he couldn't allow the corporation to operate along those lines, and he had thrown himself into the thick of the day-to-day operations in an attempt to make major changes, including replacing several key people who hadn't taken kindly to his management style. He was left with a constantly busy schedule and very little time for himself. His working summers at the family compound were very important for his peace of mind and sanity.

After filling his lungs with the clean ocean air, he exhaled with an audible sigh. Fred was right. He had to start delegating the workload. He knew he couldn't continue to carry the brunt of it without burning out. He returned to his office, settled into his chair and grabbed the project file he had been working on when Terry arrived. A few minutes later he heard the outer door open and close when Kim left to continue with the work items on her list.

A bit of a grin tugged at the corners of his mouth. It was obvious she resented the menial tasks, but it really was a great help to him to have someone to take care of those details. Normally Fred would do that type of errand, but Jared had the caretaker busy with a very time-consuming project. Fred was only at the estate for a few hours early each morning.

He had Fred overseeing a special project for him through the nonprofit organization he had formed after taking over Stevens Enterprises. He was having a new community center built on a piece of land he owned in downtown Otter Crest. It would be a place where senior citizens could gather, civic groups could hold meetings and youth groups could participate in activities. On several occasions different groups had proposed a community center funded by private money, but each group had put personal restrictions on its use. Jared wanted it to be a place everyone could use without anyone's personal bias interfering. When it was completed, he would hire a managing director to run the facility through his nonprofit organization.

It was one of those things Jared tried to keep quiet. He

didn't like sharing his philanthropic activities with outsiders. An odd thought struck him. Kim was an outsider but she didn't feel like one. It was a disturbing thought.

Kim carried three memos into Jared's office and placed them on his desk. "That's the last of it." She glanced at her watch. "It's six o'clock. I'm going home now."

Jared looked up from his work. "It's six o'clock already?" He stood and stretched in an obvious attempt to work out the kinks from sitting too long. "I haven't even had lunch yet."

"You haven't?" His admission surprised her. He had been so dedicated to his work schedule that he hadn't taken time to eat—certainly not the action of an irresponsible playboy who was nothing more than a corporate front man.

Jared cocked his head and stared at her for a moment. "It didn't work out last night, but I'm willing to try again. Would you stay and have some dinner with me tonight?"

"I, uh…" His question had caught her off guard.

"You're not going to try and tell me that you've suddenly remembered a previous commitment, are you?"

"I…no, I wasn't going to say that." She couldn't think of any reason to turn down his invitation. To tell him she didn't want to have dinner with him would be a lie of monumental proportions, but the prospect made her uneasy, especially in light of what had happened the previous night. That uneasiness, however, did not stop her curiosity about him.

Then a wave of panic hit her. He was too sexy, too desirable…way too tempting. If he made a pass at her again, would she have the emotional strength to turn him down a second time?

Jared's words cut into her thoughts, his voice edged with

hesitation. "Am I correct in interpreting your silence as an acceptance of my dinner invitation?"

"Well…I suppose it wouldn't hurt—"

"Good." He flashed a pleased grin as he indicated the hallway to the main part of the house. "I have a bottle of wine I've been saving for a special occasion. I'd like for you to share it with me. I'll get it from the wine cellar and start the charcoal while you feed Lurch."

A quick shove of irritation tried to grab her, then she shook her head in resignation as it was immediately replaced by the amusement she could not suppress. He had done it to her again…dangled the attractive treat in front of her and then when she reached for it he had added something less appetizing to the mix. Although his words about sharing a special bottle of wine continued to circulate through her mind, she wasn't sure what to make of them.

She turned toward the dog, who had been sitting patiently by her desk. "Come on, Lurch. Let's go get dinner."

At the sound of his name, the Saint Bernard jumped to attention and followed.

While Jared was in the wine cellar, Kim took out the large bag of dog food, filled Lurch's food dish and checked his water bowl. The dog immediately attacked his dinner as if he hadn't eaten in days. Kim watched him for a minute, then glanced toward the open door to the wine cellar. Her curiosity prompted her to descend the stairs. She had never been in a real wine cellar. She had seen basements where people stored wine in racks, but never the genuine thing.

At the bottom of the stairs she was disappointed to see that it was just a typical basement with storage shelves, the central heating system and the water heater. Then she noticed the room to her left, with a light on. She peered through the partially open door into the paneled room, where she saw hundreds of bottles of wine stored in wooden racks with many more bottles in temperature-controlled cabinets. She glanced around the room, then tentatively stepped inside.

"How do you like it?"

Kim spun at the sound of Jared's voice. He appeared from behind one of the racks. She felt her embarrassment flush hot across her cheeks.

"I'm sorry...I didn't mean to intrude. It's...well, I've never been in a real wine cellar before, and I wanted to see what one looked like. I hope you don't mind."

He crossed the room as he spoke. "Not at all. I'm always happy to show off my wine cellar. I had it built two years ago."

"It's very nice. How many bottles of wine do you have here?"

He reached her side as he continued to speak. "Several hundred. Actually, more than I really need to have. Each time I come across a new wine I like I end up buying several cases of it. That's definitely overkill for one person, but I do hold numerous business functions and dinners here at various times of the year, and a lot of the wine is used for that."

A tremor ran through Kim's body. His nearness was more intoxicating than all the bottles of wine in the room. It was a temptation that was almost too strong to resist. As much as she wanted to move away from him, she also wanted physical contact with him. Once again the thought popped into her mind about Jared holding her in his arms, kissing her until every inch of her body tingled with excitement...making passionate love to her.

Her decidedly erotic thoughts burst into a flame of desire when she felt his hand on her arm. His fingertips trailed

softly across her cheek before twining in her hair. He lowered his face to hers, then brushed his lips softly against
her mouth. She tried to summon some inner strength, at
least enough to stop what was beginning to feel like a very
successful seduction. As much as she wanted it to continue,
she didn't dare allow it to happen. The last thing she needed
was to be a willing participant in another of his toe-curling
kisses.

He moved closer to her. She closed her eyes in an effort
to shut out the image of this all too tempting man. But she
might as well have been trying to hold back the ocean's
tides for all the good it did.

Five

Jared felt the tension in Kim's body as he stroked her cheek. Her skin felt as smooth and creamy as it looked. Her hair was the quality of the finest golden silk. What was there about this woman that inflamed his desires beyond the point of reason? He wanted to make love to her—to taste her skin, touch every place that excited her, intimately know every inch of her body and then get to know it all over again. He slid his hand around to her nape and gently drew her head toward him as he brushed his lips against hers.

A moment later her body stiffened, her eyes popped open and she took two quick steps backward, putting herself out of his immediate reach. He saw the uncertainty in her eyes and the apprehension that covered her features. A wave of disappointment washed through him. As much as he wanted to pursue what he had started, he didn't want to create an awkward ongoing situation.

He reached out, lightly touched her cheek for a brief moment, then withdrew his hand. He searched the depths of her eyes, took a calming breath and shifted his gaze from her beautiful features and far too tempting mouth.

He responded to her unspoken words. "You're right, we need to pay attention to dinner." He pulled the bottle of wine from the rack and gestured toward the stairs.

After a few uncomfortable minutes they settled into the preparation of dinner. Jared opened the bottle of wine, then put the steaks on the grill while Kim made a salad. Initial conversation was polite but strained. When everything had been dished up and they were about to sit down, he caught her hand and pulled her toward him. His voice was soft, his words caressing her cheek.

"I really enjoy these long summer days where daylight lingers into the evening. It looks like it's going to be a beautiful sunset. Let's take dinner out onto the deck."

Jared placed both plates on a tray along with two glasses and the bottle of wine. They went from the informal dining room through the sliding glass doors to the deck. He placed everything on the table, then indicated a chair for Kim. He poured them each a glass of wine.

Jared held up his glass. "Here's to a productive summer." He paused, his glass raised, as he cocked his head and gave her a questioning look. "And to an educational one?"

Kim wrinkled her brow. "An educational one?"

"An opportunity to learn something about each other…and maybe put aside some of the old issues of a family feud that have no relationship to us or apply to our generation?"

He clinked his glass against hers, then took a drink of his wine. The glow of the setting sun highlighted her golden hair and made her blue eyes sparkle. He had never seen anyone more beautiful than she was at that moment. He watched as she hesitated as if unsure what to do, then followed his lead and took a sip of wine.

Kim set her glass on the table. It would have served no purpose to take exception to his statement about trying to put aside some of the issues of the long-standing feud between their families. In fact, it would have been petty on her part to do so. But her skepticism made her suspicious of his motives. What was he really after? Was it just another ploy by a Stevens to take advantage of a Donaldson? Lull her into a sense of security, then play out his underhanded scheme? She hoped not, but experience, history and her father's constant harangues told her she could not dismiss the possibility.

Kim's gaze drifted to the horizon. It was, indeed, going to be a beautiful sunset. Streaks of red and gold filled the sky, enhanced by the sound of crashing waves on the sand. The city lights had started to come on, ringing the edge of the bay like sparkling diamonds. Dozens of small lights twinkled along the edge of the deck railing. The underwater lights in the pool sent a shimmering flow across the water's surface. She leaned back in her chair, closed her eyes and took in a deep breath.

Everything about Jared had her confused. Nothing had gone as she had anticipated it would. He hadn't actually lied to her, but he had most certainly manipulated her with half truths and veiled deceptions. And a man like that couldn't be trusted no matter how handsome and sexy he was...no matter how much he made her pulse race and her heart pound with excitement.

She opened her eyes and nervously cleared her throat. "What's on your agenda for me to do tomorrow?" She quickly took another sip of wine. She had come within a breath of asking what tedious little errands he had in mind for her, but quickly realized that it would not be an appropriate question under the circumstances. He had opened the forum of the feud, of setting aside some of the long-held beliefs. If it had been an olive branch of sorts, she would be out of line in not responding to it.

"I haven't put together a list yet. Why don't we postpone any business discussions until the morning? For this evening, I'd rather talk about you."

"Me? There's nothing interesting about me." She nibbled at her salad as she tried to cover the embarrassment his statement caused.

Jared took a couple of bites of his steak as he studied her. "I wouldn't say that. For instance, why did you decide on teaching as a career? There are certainly lots of career paths that would be far more financially lucrative than teaching."

She stiffened in her chair, her indignation rising to the occasion. "I don't believe that money is the all-important factor in life. There are other things to consider when seeking a fulfilling occupation."

"You're right." He ignored her tone, maintaining an upbeat attitude. "Money is not the be-all and end-all of life. But that doesn't answer my question."

His quick agreement to her statement took her by surprise. It was totally out of character for the person she had painted him to be. She tried to provide an answer that would convey her true feelings.

"I find teaching very satisfying. I like the challenge it provides and the emotional fulfillment when I can see a student conquer something that has been a problem for him or achieve recognition for hard work. And I enjoy it. I like to think that I can make a difference in their lives, help them to achieve their potential."

He regarded her thoughtfully over the rim of his wineglass as he took a drink. Even in the rapidly fading daylight he could see her nervousness, but he also saw the glow of contentment in her eyes as she talked about teaching. It was obviously important to her, something she found gratifying.

He reached across and put his hand on top of hers. "I admire your dedication and purpose. How fortunate you are to have been able to find your place in life as early as you did and to be so certain about it."

As the last remnants of daylight disappeared, some of the outside lights came on, casting a soft glow across the table. She was very aware of his hand on hers but did not pull away from his touch. Something about his tone and the expression on his face touched her emotions more than she wanted it to. She cocked her head as she stared at him. "That's a rather sad statement. Does it mean that you don't find any of this—" she gestured with her free hand, indicating the lavish surrounding "—fulfilling for you? That you don't enjoy having all this at your disposal?"

Was this yet another glimpse behind the facade of a man she was finding more complex with each passing hour? Perhaps an insight into a character that truly baffled her? She wasn't sure. Was she letting her physical attraction to him offset what she thought she knew to be true of his character? She was becoming less sure about what she thought she knew.

"Sure, I enjoy the money and what it can buy. But it's not what life should be about."

"Then perhaps—" she withdrew her hand from his as her voice took on a sharp edge "—you should do something with your money beside indulging yourself."

He showed no reaction to her pointed barb other than a slight narrowing of his eyes, but she immediately berated herself. It was a stupid thing to have said and totally uncalled for. She wasn't even sure why she said it. She wasn't jealous, but could it be she resented him for what he had? What should have been her grandfather's and her father's?

She missed the warmth of his touch even though she was the one who pulled away. "I…I'm sorry. I didn't mean for that to sound the way it did. It's certainly none of my business what you do with your money."

"That's all right. No harm done."

She heard it in his voice. He may have verbally dismissed her comments as inconsequential, but he had not eliminated them from his mind. "I'm sorry…really. I had no right to say that."

Her voice dropped to a whisper. "I don't even know why I said it." Were her words and actions nothing more than a defensive reaction to a desire to be with him? She wasn't sure. She wasn't sure of anything anymore.

"Don't worry about it."

The soft light played across his handsome features, sending a wave of desire coursing through her veins. She didn't know how to respond to his words or what to do about the sensual pull he exerted on her, so she concentrated her thoughts and conversation on an area where she did have some control.

"This is an excellent wine, and the steak is delicious."

"Thank you. I'm glad you're enjoying it."

"And you were right about having dinner out here. The view is beautiful." Inane words…mindless chitchat. The awkwardness of the situation permeated the air. And she knew she was responsible for creating that awkwardness. Yet underneath that was a tingling layer of sensual desire that was drawing her closer and closer to him. She was growing more uncomfortable as the sexual tension increased.

Again she wondered what it would be like to make love

with Jared Stevens. She had never been in the inner sanctum of a true playboy's lair. Her thoughts turned to their bodies entwined on what she imagined were the silk sheets adorning his king-size bed. Her bare skin touching his along the length of his nude torso. Her fingers caressing his broad shoulders. She became aware of her breathing. If the thrill of his kiss was a sample of his skills, it would be an experience of a lifetime.

"Tell me what you know about this feud that our families have been engaged in for several decades now."

His words interrupted her thoughts, sending a wave of relief through her body. She didn't like where those thoughts had been headed, thoughts bordering on the erotic, and hadn't been able to control them. But the subject he had chosen caused her body to stiffen and her jaw to tighten.

"I'd rather not discuss it. All my life I've heard about this feud. It ruined my grandfather's life. It ruined by father's life. It made my childhood miserable. I want to bury it." She leveled a serious look at him, took a steadying breath, then asked him what was on her mind. "Why do you insist on pursuing it?"

He reached out and took her hand again and offered her a soft, sincere smile. "I think we may have found something to agree on. I want to put it behind me, too. Whatever happened is over and done and can't be changed. It's in the past, and the sins of past generations should be left there."

He felt it in the air, the sizzle and crackle of sexual energy that filled the space between them. He could still taste her on his lips. He wanted more of her, yet every time he made an advance he ended up backing off rather than pursuing what he wanted. What was there about this woman that made her so different from all the others?

There was one thing he had been able to discern about Kim Donaldson. She would never be receptive to a casual affair based on nothing more than physical desire, and there certainly was no way he would ever be interested in anything that hinted at a commitment. He would never allow his emotions to be involved, at least not any emotions beyond lust. She was just the type who could trap a less resourceful and savvy man into some sort of commitment that would end up ruining the rest of his life. That was not for him. The example of his father's many marriages and affairs had shown him that a committed relationship wasn't worth the trouble to try and make it work. So why did he still want to pursue her? He gave her hand a little squeeze, then brought it to his lips and kissed the inside of her wrist.

The uncomfortable tension based on an adversarial conflict had been broken. It was as if a weight had been lifted from her shoulders when she heard his simple and heartfelt statement about wanting to put the feud behind them.

He held up his wineglass and looked questioningly at her. "To the end of the feud?"

She clinked the rim of her glass against his. "To the end of the feud." They each took a drink to seal the pledge.

For the rest of the evening they settled into conversation about personal likes and dislikes…travel, movies, books, television. Jared turned on the stereo so the music would filter to the deck from the house. He stood, took her hand in his and coaxed her out of her chair. Then he pulled her into his arms and moved to the soft strains of the music. The previous tension and stress melted away as they became more comfortable with each other—except for the sexual tension that jumped into high gear, sizzling through the air and crackling like electrical lines on a foggy night.

It was Kim who reluctantly made the move to put an end

to the evening. "It's getting late. I should be going home. Thank you for dinner. It was very nice."

Jared took her hand as they walked into the house and continued to the front door. "It was my pleasure. Thank you for sharing it with me. I enjoyed the opportunity to be able to talk without guarding every word."

They lingered at the front door, a soft feeling of sensual warmth permeating the air. He pulled her into his arms and brushed a soft kiss against her lips, then fully claimed her mouth. He may have intended it to be a simple kiss, but a second later the full force of his passion took control of his actions. Everything about her excited him. He wanted more of her...he wanted all of her.

His kiss deepened. He brushed his tongue against hers, the texture and sensation adding to his already heated desires. He held her tighter, her body pressing against his. The rise and fall of her breasts matched his labored breathing. She was everything a man could want.

His breath tickled her ear as he whispered the soft words, "Stay the night with me."

Myriad thoughts and feelings swept through her mind, not the least of which was her repeated fantasy of making love with Jared Stevens. Did she dare surrender to his invitation? Was there any way she could be anything more to him than just another sexual conquest? Somewhere in the back of her mind she latched on to the conscious realization that her concerns told her how much she had already allowed herself to become emotionally involved with him. She had to put a stop to it before she started falling in love with him...if it wasn't already too late.

"No...I don't think that's a good idea. I should...I need to go home. I'll see you in the morning." A somewhat shaken Kim Donaldson hurried out the front door.

Jared watched as she drove down the driveway. It was

the second night in a row he had stood at his front door watching her drive away. This time, however, they had parted without anger. Far from it. His breathing might have slowed to normal, but his body still surged with unfulfilled desires.

He closed and locked the front door, then slowly walked down the hall to his bedroom. Confusion ran rampant through his mind. There was no doubt he wanted her more than he had ever wanted another woman, but he was very unsettled about exactly why and for what. Was he looking for a casual liaison? A summer affair? Some sort of arrangement that would be for a longer term? Or was it more…much more? The question frightened him almost as much as the possible answer that he refused to acknowledge.

Kim paused at the curb across the street from the entrance gates to Jared's house. She had spent another long and troublesome night with her emotions in turmoil. Dinner with Jared had been enchanting, and once the animosities had been set aside she found there was much more to him than a killer smile, devastatingly good looks and an easy charm. She had been given a peek into the inner workings of this man, a depth of character she had not known was there. He had turned out to be someone she truly wanted to be with, but was wanting anything more than what they had already shared merely asking for trouble? She didn't know what to think. With a sigh, she drove around to the office entrance. The confusion continued to swirl in her head.

As soon as she entered the office Jared pulled a startled Kim into his arms. His voice was soft, warm and inviting.

"Good morning."

A moment later his mouth found hers. It was a brief kiss,

but hot enough to sizzle her senses and curl her toes. It ignited all the embers of passion that still smoldered from the previous night.

She managed to force out some words. "This isn't getting any work done."

"But it's much more fun." He stole one more quick kiss before relinquishing her tempting presence from his arms.

Jared had several things for her to do, most of them keeping her in the office rather than out running simple little errands. Kim was pleased to find that her work assignments included more serious tasks, some of them involving his clients and current business functions. She took it as a gesture of trust that touched her on the deepest levels.

Things between them grew more comfortable with each passing day. Jared surprised her one noon with a picnic lunch in the backyard. As the week went by they settled into getting to know each other as friends rather than adversaries—something beyond the underlying sexual tension that continued to pull at each of them with passion-filled kisses whenever they were together and sensual fantasies when they were apart.

Even though Jared continued to ask her to spend the night and she yearned to have him make love to her, she had steadfastly maintained her need to go home. She knew she was afraid, but wasn't sure exactly why. Was it the thought of all the other women Jared had wooed and bedded? Was it her concern that he would think she considered making love just a game without taking the implications seriously? Was it her fear that he would think of it as nothing more than a game? Or was it that she suspected she was falling in love with him and didn't want to be? It had turned into an ongoing battle between her desires and her fears.

One week turned into two and two became four. By the

end of the month she was so confused in her feelings for Jared she hardly knew which way to turn. Every time he touched her, waves of sensual desire swept through her body. And each night as she went to bed alone at her father's house she wondered how much longer she could hold out against Jared's subtle seduction and her own not-so-subtle desires.

Friday evening finally arrived. Kim finished her work for the week and put her desk in order, preparing to leave for the weekend. Jared had asked her to wait until he returned from a business meeting with his bankers in San Francisco. She glanced at her watch but didn't know what time to expect him. She decided to feed Lurch while she waited. She assumed Jared had asked her to wait so they could do something together that night, maybe dinner out. She had dressed in teal blue silk pants and blouse with her favorite gold necklace anticipating they would go somewhere nice since he had dressed in suit and tie for his meeting.

She returned to the office just as Jared arrived. There was no doubt about how handsome and dynamic he was. Her heart beat a little faster, and her blood coursed hot through her veins. The added dimension of the custom-tailored charcoal gray suit, silk shirt with French cuffs and gold cuff links and the charcoal gray Gucci loafers said the man standing in front of her was powerful, wealthy and a force to be reckoned with.

"Kim...I've been thinking about something and I want to discuss it with you."

"What is it?"

He knew he hadn't been fair in giving her so many menial little tasks and errands the first few days, even though the month had settled into a smooth running working relationship with her spending most of her time in the office. He needed to do something about the charity fund-raiser his client wanted him to organize. He had been putting it off, but the more he thought about it, the more it seemed like a perfect project to give to Kim. It would be a great help to him. It would be something they could work on together. It would also keep her at his house for long days, perhaps long hours that would extend late into the night.

"How are you at planning fund-raising events?"

"Fund-raising events?" His question caught her by surprise. "What kind of fund-raising events?"

"You know...food, drinks, dancing and entertainment followed by the solicitation of large checks payable to the charity. Just your typical run-of-the-mill type of fund-raiser attended by the socially prominent and business elite."

"Which charity are you talking about?"

"Well..." He ran his hand across the back of his neck. "I don't recall the name of the organization, but it has to do with shelters for battered women and abused children. It's the favorite charity of the wife of one of our biggest clients. I'm sort of on the hook to put on a fund-raising event for them and I was considering just hiring a service to handle it, but if that's something you know about, perhaps you could help me with it. If I didn't have to hire a service it would cut down on the expenses of putting on the event and leave more of the money for the charity." He paused long enough to pull her hair aside and place a tender kiss behind her ear. "We could work on it together."

A shiver of delight darted across her skin. "I do have a little bit of experience in event planning. I've been in charge of a couple of fund-raisers at the high school where I teach, but that's pretty far removed from the socially prominent and business elite."

His smile lit up his face, that devilishly sexy smile that never failed to set her heart a-flutter. "That sounds good enough to me. I think we can consider that your primary assignment for the rest of the summer. I'd like to hold the function in San Francisco in September or early October at one of the major hotel ballrooms.''

She couldn't hide her elation. ''You want me to work on this with you? To plan and organize a function of this size and importance?''

''Yes, I have confidence in your ability to handle it.'' He held her eye contact for a long moment, his smile fading and a new depth of intensity filling his eyes.

His request was totally unexpected. The change from menial little errands the first few days to helping plan a major charity fund-raising event just a month later was a huge leap in responsibility. His words settled a soft glow of pleasure over her. He had said he had confidence in her and they would be working on the project together.

This was certainly different from the passionate kisses and lingering touches they had shared over the past few weeks. It was much more than his attempts to get her to stay the night at his house. She experienced a shortness of breath caused as much by the excitement of the charity project and his obvious trust and confidence in her abilities as by the sensual warmth spreading through her veins.

She tried to force calm into her voice. ''When do you want me to start on the charity project?''

''If you don't mind, maybe we could start work on it in the morning? I know you aren't supposed to work on Saturday, but it will give us an opportunity to work without interruptions. We can at least get a feel for what needs to be done.''

''That's fine. I don't mind working Saturday morning.'' Her excitement over the new project continued to tingle through her body.

''I have a few pamphlets about the charity. I think

they're on the coffee table in the living room. Come on, you can look them over before we start work on it."

Kim followed Jared to the living room. She looked around, her gaze moving from one beautiful object to another. She recalled when she had glimpsed this room from the entryway upon her arrival for her first day of work. A full week had gone by before she could actually take in the magnificent surroundings.

He crossed the room to the coffee table and picked up the brochures. "Here—" he held them out to her "—this should give you information about the background and current organization of the charity."

She took the material, but before she could say or do anything else he grasped her other hand and brought it to his lips. He captured her gaze and held it as he kissed her palm.

"My offer for you to stay the night is still open."

She shook her head. She finally forced out a breathless word. "Please..." Her resistance to his charms weakened with each breath she took, aided by her desire. "I really can't. The real estate agent is holding an open house on Sunday. I need to make sure everything is in order. I need to sell my father's house." Did he have any idea how tempting his offer was? How much she wanted to stay the night with him? And not just because he had dangled a challenging project under her nose, either.

"I think you should stay." Jared gave her hand a squeeze. It was precisely the intimate gesture of reassurance she needed. A moment later his mouth was on hers, and the last of her resistance evaporated. The desires she had been fighting for the past month, ever since she met him, had finally won. She circled her arms around his neck, allowing the brochures to fall to the floor, and returned his passion with an equal amount of her own. Whatever objection she might have had no longer mattered. Her resolve melted in his arms.

The moment she put her arms around his neck a hard jolt of something unexpected hit Jared like a bolt of lightning. His libido had been in overdrive from their first meeting, but now she touched far more than his sensual desires. She touched a place so deep inside him he wasn't even sure exactly where it was.

And he wasn't sure he wanted to know.

He cupped her face in his hands. His words came out in a husky whisper. "Do you have any idea how beautiful and desirable you are?"

Before she could answer, he brought his mouth down on hers as he wrapped her in his embrace. He pulled her body tightly to him. His lips nibbled at the corners of her mouth, then he twined his tongue with hers. With one hand he ran his fingers through the silky strands of her hair before caressing her shoulders. The other hand slid across her hip and cupped the roundness of her bottom. He snuggled her hips against his.

His fingers made their way to the top button of her blouse. He paused to kiss the bare skin exposed each time a button slipped through a buttonhole until her blouse was completely unfastened. He ran his hands inside her blouse, caressing the smooth skin of her back, then unhooking her bra. He removed both garments, dropping them to the floor.

A little shiver darted across her skin as the cool air hit her body, but it was quickly replaced by the warmth of his arms as he enfolded her in his embrace again. She slipped her feet out of her shoes and kicked them aside. There wasn't any use pretending that nothing was going to happen or trying to convince herself she could put a stop to what was taking place. She wanted Jared to make love to her more than she had ever wanted anything in her life. Even her fingertips tingled at the thought of running her hands over his bare skin.

She loosened his tie and pulled it from around his neck, then dropped it to the floor. Her fingers worked at the buttons on his shirt until they were unfastened. She slid her hands inside his shirt, reveling in the hard planes of his chest. She felt his breathing, the ragged intake matching her own. His mouth was on hers again—hot, demanding and tantalizingly sensual. But he didn't demand any more than she was willing to give. He interrupted the kiss just long enough to yank his shirt off and toss it on the floor on top of his tie.

He kicked off his shoes and took a couple of steps backward, taking her with him as he fell onto the sofa. He leaned into the corner, holding her body on top of his as he caressed her bare shoulders and back. His tongue meshed with hers, exploring the dark recesses of her mouth. Their legs tangled together. The feel of her bare breasts pressing against his chest sent a heated surge through his body. His hardened arousal strained against the front of his trousers.

His words were barely audible. "You are exquisite." He twisted so his body covered hers, one of his legs between hers and the other hanging over the edge of the sofa. He cupped the firmness of her breast, her tautly puckered nipple pressing into his hand. He captured her other nipple in his mouth. A soft moan of pleasure filled the air. He didn't know if it had come from him or from her. Perhaps it was from both of them.

Her hands were at his trousers, trying to unfasten his belt and unzip his pants. He reached for the waist of her slacks. Their hands collided as each frantically tugged at the other's remaining pieces of clothing. Jared released her nipple from his mouth and raised up on his elbows. He gasped for air and finally managed a few breathless words.

"Let's go to my bedroom."

He rolled off the sofa, his chest heaving with his labored breathing. He grabbed her hand and pulled her to her feet. Then he impulsively scooped her in his arms, carried her up the stairs to his bedroom and laid her on the bed. He gulped in several deep breaths as he shucked off his trousers, socks and briefs.

Kneeling on the bed, he unfastened her slacks as quickly as his trembling hands could function. She arched her hips upward, allowing him to pull them off along with her panty hose and lacy bikini panties. He stared at the beautiful woman who had dominated all his thoughts from the time he met her. Her slightly parted kiss-swollen lips and mussed hair gave her an earthy look of wild abandon and exotic sensuality. Her blue eyes sparkled with the same passion that coursed hotly through his veins. She raised her hand toward him, beckoning him to join her.

The last vestige of control he had been able to muster flew out the window. He snuggled his body next to hers. He teased her nipple with the tip of his tongue before drawing it in and gently suckling. Her mouth…her skin…every touch and taste inflamed his senses. He ran his hand up the smooth skin of her inner thigh until he reached the moist heat of her femininity.

A gasp followed by a sensual moan of pleasure escaped Kim's throat when he inserted his finger between her feminine folds. She splayed her fingers across his hard chest, then trailed her fingertips down his body. She stroked his hardened arousal, the sensual delight sending a wave of excitement through her body that rapidly combined with the strong sensations produced by his touch.

She wrapped her leg around his, threw her head back

into the pillow, closed her eyes and allowed the delicious waves of euphoria to surge through her body. A moment later his mouth came down hard on hers. She circled her arms around his neck. His hot kiss infused her with an intense sexuality that emanated from his every breath and gesture. No one had ever set her passions on fire the way he did.

Jared reached for the drawer of the nightstand and withdrew the condom packet, his movements almost frantic in his rush to rip open the package. A few moments later he nestled his body between her legs and slowly thrust his manhood inside her. He held her tightly as a hard jolt of something as emotional as it was physical claimed every corner of his consciousness. He fought to keep the emotional side of what was happening under control. He set a smooth pace, each of his strokes being met by a thrust of Kim's hips. His mouth captured hers again, as much in an attempt to prevent him from saying more than he wanted to as it was a need for the intimate contact and a desire to experience her taste.

Kim's emotions vied for control with the physical rush surging through her body. Everything about Jared excited her more than she believed it could...every place he touched her, every word he said. The pace of their lovemaking accelerated as layer upon layer of intense rapture built toward the ultimate ecstasy. She tightened her arms around him. His kiss demanded more, and she gave everything she could until the convulsions totally claimed her body in a climactic euphoria more intense than anything she had ever experienced. She clung to him as the waves surged through her again and again. It had been everything she knew it would be, everything she had anticipated...and more.

Jared wavered between wanting to prolong the delicious

sensations and giving in to the rapture that rushed to claim him. He gave one final deep thrust. His body shuddered, followed by hard spasms of release. There was so much he wanted to say, and every bit of it frightened him more than anything in his life ever had.

Jared kissed Kim's damp cheek, brushed his lips tenderly against hers and continued to hold her. He didn't want to let go of her warmth or break the physical contact that continued to radiate to him.

He had been with women who immediately wanted praise for their performance, to be told that they were beautiful and desirable and that it was the best lovemaking he had ever experienced. Others wanted him to make a commitment to a relationship, even though he had made no such promises or even hinted at the possibility. Others felt a need to tell him about their lovers in an attempt to impress him with their vast experience. He hadn't been interested in any of it.

But Kim was different. She didn't do any of those things. She seemed strangely quiet, as if there were many thoughts going through her mind, secrets she chose not to share. It left him very uneasy and at a loss about what to do or say to her. A wave of apprehension jittered through his body and flowed into the one area where he had no experience— a previously unknown insecurity.

Making love had never before had an emotional impact on him the way it had with Kim. Every fear he had ever harbored about commitment and relationships, every negative thought he had ever held about his father's many failed marriages, came rushing at him. Foreign feelings coursed through him, feelings that frightened him…feelings that told him to run before it was too late.

Feelings that told him it was already too late.

So he continued to hold her tightly while he tried to convince himself that nothing had changed, that everything was okay even though he knew things would never be the same again.

Kim remained folded in his embrace, the glow of total contentment resonating through every fiber of her being. Before they had made love she suspected she might be falling in love with him. Now she knew it for sure. What she didn't know was how she felt about the revelation. He was the type of man whose lifestyle and existence shouted for all to hear that he would never allow himself to be tied down to one woman in a committed relationship.

Could she be happy as his lover knowing she could never be anything more? One thing was definite—whatever relationship existed between them before they made love, even if it was only a contracted work arrangement, had been irrevocably changed.

What just moments ago had been total elation was suddenly dampened by so many doubts and fears. Had she done something she would live to regret? She hoped not, but she feared so.

Jared kissed her cheek, drawing her out of her thoughts. Then he nuzzled her neck as he caressed her breast. A renewed tingle of excitement quickly made its way through her body. He slowly tickled his fingers up her inner thigh, and she was once again poised on the brink of a rapturous experience.

It was another hour before they basked in the afterglow of their intense lovemaking for a second time. If Jared had been uncertain earlier about where the impact of their lovemaking would lead, now he was in a state of total confusion. He wrapped his arms tightly around Kim's body and held her to him. Maybe things would be clearer in the morning. He closed his eyes and tried to put the negative thoughts out of his mind while gently stroking her skin.

Kim delighted in the little tremors of excitement that followed in the wake of his fingertips. She had never felt so at one with another human being as she did at that moment. How was it possible for Jared to become so important to her, so much the emotional center of her existence in only a month? She snuggled into the comfort and security of his arms. Her thoughts became fewer and less clear as sleep claimed her.

Six

Jared sat on the edge of the bed watching Kim as she slept. He had slipped out of bed half an hour earlier to make coffee and bring in the morning newspaper. Conflicting thoughts and feelings ran rampant through him. On the one hand he wanted to be with her, to share everything with her. Even the possibility of building a life together had entered his thoughts. She was unlike any woman he had ever known. Just looking at her sent a shiver through his body, telling him of the magnitude of the impact their love-making had on him. It had never seemed so important on every level of existence as it had with Kim.

But on the other hand, he felt as if the walls were closing in on him, trapping him in something he wasn't ready for. He wanted to stay as much as he instinctively wanted to run. Nothing had ever put him into a state of inner turmoil the way this had. And he had been totally unprepared for it.

His pulse raced a little faster and his heartbeat pounded a little harder as he took in the beautiful woman sleeping in his bed. He reached out and lightly stroked her hair, brushing errant strands from the side of her face. Her long, dark lashes rested against her upper cheek. He watched the gentle rise and fall of her breasts corresponding with her slow, even breathing. His gaze traced the enticing curve of her hip and her long, shapely legs. She stirred, then stretched her arms and legs.

Kim slowly opened her eyes. The first sight that greeted her was Jared's face. She smiled. "Good morning." A soft warmth spread through her body as she recalled the intensity of their lovemaking and the heat of the passion between them. "Have you been awake for long?"

"No…just long enough to make some coffee." He wanted to touch her, to feel the silky smoothness of her skin and experience the sensual oneness of the physical contact with her. He started to reach out, but withdrew his hand. He didn't know why. A sudden jolt of panic gripped him and refused to let go. He stood and walked to the other side of the bed.

"I brought your clothes up from the living room."

A hint of a frown creased her forehead. "Thank you." A million warning bells went off inside her head. There was something different about him, but she couldn't put her finger on exactly what it was. Was his attitude a little cooler? His manner a bit more formal? He hadn't kissed her, not even the gesture of touching her cheek as he had numerous times over the past month. A little chill darted across her skin. She pulled the sheet up to cover her even though she knew the chill was emotional rather than physical.

She had wondered the night before if she would regret her decision to make love with Jared. Had that decision already come back to haunt her, or were her fears preying on her insecurities? She reached for the clothes he had placed on the foot of the bed. Was it his way of telling her he wanted her to leave even though it had been previously agreed that they would work on the charity project that day? Had *he* been struck with regrets?

A shudder of apprehension attached itself to her fears. She was no good at the morning after game of vying for the upper hand to control what was happening. She would relieve him of the decision by making the first move and taking the matter out of his hands.

"I'm going to go home so I can take a shower and put on some clean clothes. Then I'll be back and we can start on the charity fund-raiser as we discussed...if that's okay with you."

"Sure, that's fine. We can have breakfast when you get back." He heard the coolness in his voice and the distance it projected but didn't seem able to prevent it. He turned away, guilt surging through his consciousness over his inability to make eye contact with her. He wanted to take her in his arms, to hold her—to tell her that he thought he might be falling in love with her. He had allowed the reality to crystallize in his mind, but it didn't resolve anything. All it did was frighten him more than he already was, if that was possible.

Kim pulled on her clothes, then ran her fingers through her mussed hair. The sick churning in the pit of her stomach said something was very wrong. Was it her imagination? Her doubts and fears? Or was it real? Her emotions were running wild, and she needed to get them under control. What minutes earlier had been a time of blissful contentment had turned into confusion and doubts. She hurried toward the front door.

"I should be back in a couple of hours." She didn't look

back to see the expression on his face, nor did she wait to hear what he might say. It was all she could do to maintain a steady walking pace rather than making a dash for her car. The churning in her stomach tried to push the sick feeling up her throat. In an almost involuntary action, she glanced at the house as she opened her car door. Jared stood on the porch, an odd expression on his face that she couldn't read.

He watched as Kim slid in behind the steering wheel and drove down the long driveway. It seemed like she had been in a great hurry to leave his house, as if she couldn't get away fast enough. Had it been his fault? Had he subconsciously pushed her away? More than anything, he had wanted to take her in his arms and make love to her all over again. But instead he had handed her clothes to her and made no effort to allay any concerns she might have had. He did nothing to reassure her that she was far more to him than just another bedmate, that he cared about her very much—perhaps too much. He had behaved like a grade A jerk. It was the type of behavior Terry would have exhibited.

He reluctantly went inside the house and closed the door. Suddenly he felt very much alone. And more than that, for the first time in his life, he truly knew what it was like to be lonely.

Lurch padded across the floor, let out a loud bark, then headed toward the kitchen. Jared followed the dog to the utility room where he filled the food dish and replenished the water bowl. Jared watched the dog for a couple of minutes as it attacked the food. "Lurch…I think I just made the biggest mistake of my life. I'll know for sure in a couple of hours when Kim returns." A wave of panic swept over him. "*If* she returns."

He tried to busy himself in his office. He pulled together

the information he had about the charity and what his clients said they wanted. He tried to keep his attention focused, but his mind kept wandering. Every few minutes his thoughts turned to Kim, to the way she felt in his arms, to the total and complete joy that assailed his senses the moment they joined together as one when they made love. He knew in the very depths of his soul that no one would ever touch his heart the way she had.

But none of that stopped the dark cloud from settling over him. The uncomfortable feeling that had made itself known when he first met her, the sensation that his life was about to take a dramatic detour from the course he had intended, had been resurrected and expanded to new dimensions. He had to grapple with the fear that churned inside him, the confusion he couldn't shake off and the anxiety that touched every corner of his conscious reality. Regardless of how much he wanted to be with Kim, the prospect of making a commitment to her was too terrifying for him. Everything he had experienced in life and witnessed growing up in his father's house told him that a commitment in a personal relationship could never work.

Stevens men could never commit for life. How could Jared think he could? He was his father's son.

Jared glanced at the clock again. Only five minutes had passed since he last checked the time. Kim had left his house almost four hours earlier, saying she would be back in a couple of hours. Had she changed her mind and decided not to return until her agreed upon regular work schedule on Monday? Had he driven a wedge between them to replace the fence they had torn down over the past month—the fence that had separated the Stevenses and Donaldsons for three generations of a family feud?

He nervously paced up and down the office, then went

to his bedroom. He stared at the rumpled bed where they had made love so passionately that every detail had become burned into his memory forever—every touch, every taste, every sensation. Would that memory have to last him a lifetime? He had never been so confused and uncertain about anything in his entire life. Perhaps he could have convinced himself that she was only a passing desire if they had not made love. But now it was too late for that.

Lurch's barking brought him out of his thoughts. Then he heard her speaking to the dog. It was as if a weight had been lifted from his shoulders but was still poised to drop on him again. She had returned, but that didn't tell him what the future held. He rushed to the office to greet her.

"You've been gone for nearly four hours. I was beginning to think you weren't coming back." He had meant the statement as one of concern, but realized when he saw her eyes narrow and her jaw tighten that it had come out as an accusation. Suddenly he couldn't do anything right where she was concerned. Once again he found himself treading on unknown territory, and the lack of any seeming control fed into the insecurity he had never experienced before meeting Kim Donaldson.

Kim straightened from where she had kneeled to greet the dog. She had hoped the rest of the day wouldn't be awkward, but it was apparently a wish that would not be fulfilled. "I needed to do some work before tomorrow's open house. I didn't want to leave it until the last minute and take a chance on not getting it done in time. It's important for me to be able to sell my father's house as quickly as possible so I can pay off the rest of his debts and settle his estate."

Her words grabbed his attention. "If you sell the house right away, where will you stay for the rest of the summer while finishing your work contract here?" He could offer her temporary housing in one of his guest rooms and then maybe…he stopped his wandering thoughts. What was he thinking? Wandering…his thoughts weren't wandering, they were galloping full force toward a situation that could only be described as the first step in making a commitment.

"I'll worry about that when the house sells. I could always commute from my apartment in San Francisco, even though it would be almost an hour drive each way. There are people who drive that kind of a commute to and from work every day."

A quick jab of disgust hit her. Her contracted work arrangement—he certainly wasn't going to let her forget about it. She took a calming breath, then walked to the desk in the reception area and picked up the file folder Jared had left there. Last night had been a horrible mistake, but she couldn't undo what had happened. All she could do was move forward in a strictly businesslike manner and try to avoid any unpleasant situations for the balance of her required summer work schedule.

And somehow she had to bury her feelings and deny what she had reluctantly admitted to herself was her love for Jared Stevens—a love that obviously would never be returned.

"What do you plan to do tomorrow while the real estate agent is holding the open house?"

"I plan to go to my apartment in San Francisco, water my plants and pack a larger suitcase with more clothes than what I brought with me. I've been living out of that suitcase for quite a while now, washing the same clothes over and over again. I'd like to wear something different for a change."

"Oh." He nervously shifted his weight from one foot to the other. "I held breakfast for you. I assumed you'd come back so we could eat together."

"I've already eaten." She looked at Jared in time to see a hint of disappointment flicker across his face.

"Where do you want to start on the charity project?" She didn't want to prolong any personal conversation. She was there strictly for business. "Do you have any ideas you want implemented? Do you want me to communicate directly with your client?"

"My client dumped the entire thing in my lap before he and his wife left for Europe. He said to let him know when everything was finalized, that he didn't really want to be bothered with any step-by-step progress reports. Everything he provided me, with regard to instructions, information, likes and dislikes, is in that file folder. So...do you have any thoughts?"

Thoughts? Yes, she had one immediate thought. Maybe this charity fund-raiser was the perfect solution to her dilemma. It would allow her to fulfill her contracted work arrangement with Jared while functioning autonomously without constant communication and the need to go to Jared for a list of menial little chores.

She pulled together her best business manner. "Well, the first thing we need to do is set a date and location for the function. We can't make any other arrangements such as hiring the caterers or an orchestra or booking any entertainment until we can tell them when and where. We can't have invitations printed and sent out until we have the when and where finalized."

"Sounds good to me. I thought maybe the ballroom of one of the large downtown San Francisco hotels."

She cocked her head in surprise. "A hotel ballroom? How large an affair did you anticipate? I had assumed it would be something you would do here."

"No...I think it would be better if we held it at a hotel. It would be closer to people's homes in town. Those who might imbibe a bit too much champagne would be able to take a cab home or stay at the hotel overnight. And it would be a location that would be able to accommodate hundreds of people, a room large enough for eating and also dancing.''

"That sounds reasonable. So, I guess my first order of business is to book the hotel facility. Did your client have any specific date in mind?''

"He suggested late September or the first of October. Since this is now the first of July, that gives us most of three months to get it together.''

"No…it gives me only two months until the first of September when my contracted work schedule is completed. After that, the last-minute details will be yours.'' Her words came out harsh, much harsher than she intended them to be. She attempted to recover and get on with the business that needed to be done today.

"Does your client have any type of a theme he wants to use?''

"A theme.'' Jared stared at her for a moment as he wrinkled his brow in concentration. "I hadn't really thought of that, and he never mentioned it. Do you have any suggestions?''

"Not at the moment, but I'll see what I can come up with. Do you want me to start work on this now or wait until Monday morning? Do you have an invitation list? I'll need to know how many people we're talking about.''

"The names for the invitation list should be available in a few days. Part of it is coming from my client's office and the other part is coming from the charity organization. There will be duplicate names between the two lists that will need to be eliminated and everything put into one master list. That will give you the maximum number to work with. I don't know what percentage of those invited usually attend this type of an affair. After all, the bottom line is the amount of checks that come in rather than the number of people who attend the fund-raiser in person.''

''Yes, but you don't want to incur a large amount of unnecessary expenses that will take away from the net amount going to the charity. If you arrange food for five hundred people and only two hundred people show up, you'll still have to pay for five hundred people.''

''You're right. I hadn't thought about that.''

''Do you have a San Francisco phone book?''

Jared pointed to the desk. ''There's one in the bottom drawer.''

''I should begin by getting price information from the hotels and I'll most likely need to wait until Monday for the right people to be at work. In fact, by using a hotel ballroom the deal would include catering and bar setup rather than needing to handle that separately. Of course, it will still require coordination with the banquet manager as far as food, drink, table decorations, flowers, valet parking and other things of that sort are concerned.''

Kim remained at the office for another three hours. She made a list of all the major hotels and their phone numbers, then she made a second list of everything she needed to discuss with the hotel to make sure she hadn't forgotten anything.

She purposely stayed busy, not looking up to see what Jared was doing or taking a break that would give them an opportunity to talk. She welcomed the busy work schedule the charity event would provide her. She welcomed having some place to focus her attention and energy so she didn't have an opportunity to think about what had happened with Jared—to think about a future without the man she had grown to love in such a short time, but a true love nonetheless. A love she now knew would not be returned.

Jared watched her as she worked. He didn't want to hover over her, but he didn't want to be very far from her, either. He tried to occupy his time by doing little chores around the house, but his thoughts kept going to Kim and an idea that had started in the back of his mind.

As the afternoon progressed he formulated a plan. He would buy her father's house, an anonymous cash transaction. That way he could insist on an immediate closing so he would have possession of the property. He would offer her the opportunity of staying in one of his guest rooms free so she could complete her summer work schedule. It would be a business arrangement, no different than her working off her father's debt. There was no reason to assume it would necessarily be a prelude to a commitment.

Jared slowly shook his head and dismissed the plan. It was an incredibly stupid idea. Even in his desperate state of mind he recognized it as a blatant attempt to manipulate her. But he had to do something, and so far everything he had done from the moment she woke up that morning had been wrong.

He had handed Kim her clothes as if to say he thought it was time for her to go home. Then, when she returned, he had been caustic in the way he had asked where she had been, as if he were criticizing her or accusing her of something. A very uneasy feeling settled inside him. His life had been totally under control and running along without any major problems until he tried to collect a long overdue debt. Now all of a sudden he didn't seem to be able to handle the simplest things without agonizing over them and then messing up anyway.

Kim Donaldson had muddled his mind, or perhaps mesmerized would be a better word. He had never had this happen before. Was this what it was like to be in love? If so, then it was too painful and he wasn't so sure he wanted anything to do with it. He clenched his jaw as he searched inside himself for some composure and determination. Buying her father's house, trying to manipulate her to get what he wanted was definitely a lousy idea.

The sounds of Kim putting the reception area in order in preparation for leaving interrupted his thoughts. He left his office to intercept her before she could get out the door. He wanted to try to smooth the feathers he had unintentionally ruffled.

"I want to thank you for working today even though it's not one of your regular workdays. It's a huge relief for me to know that the fund-raiser is in capable hands and will be properly taken care of."

"Uh, thank you."

He heard her hesitation and saw the uncertainty in her eyes. He didn't know what else to say. Perhaps things would be better when Monday morning arrived.

They had made love and then he had done the last thing he wanted to do and the worst possible thing he could have done. Instead of drawing her closer, he had put a wall between them. And now he had to figure out how to tear down that wall and repair the damage he had done.

"I'll see you Monday morning?"

"Sure." Kim didn't know what to make of Jared's attitude. First he had practically told her to get out of his bed and go home. Then he had a very accusatory tone to his voice when he questioned why she had been gone so long. And now he seemed to be wanting to make it up to her, but hadn't said anything about it.

She was very confused. Perhaps things would look better on Monday morning. She grabbed her purse and left his house.

Seven

The insistent ringing of the phone finally penetrated Kim's sleep and roused her to consciousness. She squinted as she stared at the clock on the nightstand. *Three o'clock in the morning? Who in the world could be calling me at this hour on a Monday morning? It's probably a wrong number...some drunk who can't find his way home. Maybe whoever it is will give up if I don't answer it.*

After three more rings she finally grabbed the receiver and managed to croak out a curt response to the intrusion. "Who is this and what do you want at this hour?"

"Get over here right now."

She sat upright and tried to shake the sleep from her mind as she attempted to make sense of the call. "Jared? Is that you?" Sarcasm enveloped her words. "Does this mean you need someone to change the channel on your television for you? Do you have any idea what time—"

"Now—I need your help right now. Hurry!"

The phone line went dead as he hung up without even saying goodbye. Kim was wide awake and angry. *How dare he insist that I come to his house in the middle of the night! Not even an explanation of why, just an order to be there. There was nothing in our letter of agreement that said he had the right to wake me up in the middle of the night and demand that I go to work. It would serve him right if I went back to sleep and ignored his demand.*

She reluctantly climbed out of bed, then stood in the middle of the room as a realization struck her. The edge in his voice seemed to be desperation more than anything else, and he had said he needed her help. Was there a genuine problem to deal with? Was he okay? Had he been injured? Was he ill? A new surge of panic rushed through Kim. He said he needed her help, and it sounded urgent. She threw on her clothes, then dashed to her car.

A few minutes later she arrived at Jared's house. Before she could ring the bell, the large double doors swung open. The sight and sound that greeted her were the last things she would have imagined.

Jared held a crying toddler in his arms. The look on his face was a clear combination of panic and stark terror.

"Do you know anything about babies?"

"I used to baby-sit a lot in high school and college."

"Good." He frantically held the noisy bundle toward her. "That makes you an expert in my book."

A startled Kim took the child from him. "Where did—"

"I changed her diaper and tried to feed her, but she won't stop crying." Jared looked at Kim, his eyes pleading as much as his tone of voice. "Can you do something? Can you make her stop crying? Crying this much can't be good for her. She'll make herself sick."

Jared wore only a pair of jeans. He was barefooted and bare-chested. His broad shoulders, hard chest and strong arms brought back memories of their lovemaking. His tousled hair made him look as if he had just climbed out of a warm bed, the same bed she had shared with him a couple of nights ago. Her heart pounded a little harder. She quickly turned her attention to the crying child, as much in an attempt to rid her mind of the erotic thoughts prompted by the sight of a half-naked Jared Stevens as it was to tend to the needs of the toddler.

"You said her. What's her name? How old is she? Whose child is she? Where did she come from?" It was quite a revelation. This very assertive, take-charge man appeared to be genuinely afraid of the noisy little girl.

Jared seemed not to hear her questions. "Can you make her stop crying? I didn't know what to do."

Kim looked around. They were standing in the doorway, the cool night air streaming in around them. She didn't see any other people, nor did she see anything that might belong to the toddler. She tried again to get Jared's attention. "Where are her parents?"

"She was given to me. That makes me responsible for her."

"Someone left this child here?" Her incredulity at what he had said came out in her voice. "What in the world are you talking about?" She kicked the front door closed and headed toward the living room, looking for a place to sit down.

"No, not there." A moment later they arrived at the den. A bit of frustration pushed at her. His thoughts and manner were totally scattered, and she didn't seem to be able to get through to him with her questions. She spotted a duffel bag next to the sofa and a blanket on the floor.

"Jared..." Kim watched as he paced up and down. She put a little more volume into her words. "Jared, could you please spread the blanket on the sofa so I can put her down?''

His head snapped up and he looked at Kim as if he had just become aware that she was in the room. ''What? Oh…the blanket…the sofa…sure.'' He did as she asked.

''What's her name?'' Kim placed the toddler on the blanket. She managed to suppress the amused chuckle that tried to escape when she saw the ludicrous way the diaper had been put on the child. Jared had definitely been way out of his element when he had tried to change the little girl.

''Her name is Chloe.''

Kim opened the duffel bag and searched through the items to see what supplies were available for taking care of Chloe. There was one small box of disposable diapers, pajamas, some cookies, a drinking cup and a raggedy teddy bear. She adjusted and fastened the diaper so it was a proper snug fit, then handed the stuffed bear to the little girl, who eagerly took it from her.

Kim sat on the edge of the sofa and held Chloe in her arms until the child had quieted down. She continued to rock her until the toddler fell asleep. Her attention was focused on the little girl, but she caught glimpses of Jared out of the corner of her eye. He was staring at her with what seemed to be a combination of admiration and gratitude. She gently placed Chloe on the blanket and pulled the other side over the child to keep her warm.

Kim stood up, took a deep breath and slowly expelled it. ''I think she's finally asleep.''

''Yes…I noticed the quiet.'' The relief echoed in his words and showed on his face. ''Thanks for your help. It never occurred to me that it would be as easy as giving her a teddy bear.''

She shot Jared a curious look. ''Well, it wasn't quite as easy as all that. She was very upset, and I'm sure she was also scared being taken from her bed in the middle of the night and handed to a complete stranger.''

Kim sat on the sofa and fixed her gaze on Jared. She saw the uneasiness in the depths of his green eyes. ''Now that you have me over here at this horrible hour, I think you owe me an explanation. What is this all about. What did you mean when you said someone *gave* Chloe to you? Who left her? Who are her parents? Why did they leave a little girl here in the middle of the night?''

Jared took a steadying breath as he ran his fingers through his dark hair. ''I'm not sure I know the complete story. I'm told that Chloe is eighteen months old.''

Kim paused as she turned the next question over in her mind before asking it. ''Are you her father?''

Jared shot her a pointed look, a combination of amusement and annoyance. ''I don't know her mother's name, but Terry is apparently her father. It was Terry who brought her here about midnight and dumped her on me.''

He slumped down on the sofa next to Kim. He leaned his head back and closed his eyes. She saw the weariness on his face, and something else that she could only interpret as a deep concern. It was yet another facet of the character of what she now knew was a very complex man. She started to reach out to smooth the worry lines on his forehead but withdrew her hand without making the desired physical contact.

She continued to watch him. His breathing became slower and deeper until he had dozed off. She reached out again, this time lightly running her fingertips across his brow.

He jerked to attention and quickly looked around as if trying to get his bearings. He fixed his gaze on Kim. ''What happened?'' He leaned back and emitted a sigh of resignation. ''Did I fall asleep?''

"I think so, but it's understandable." She paused, hoping he would continue with his explanation of why Chloe was there. When he didn't say anything she prompted him for more information.

"You were telling me how all of this happened."

He gestured toward the sleeping child. "Yeah...all of this."

Jared rose and slowly approached the other end of the sofa. He stood over Chloe and watched her for a moment before turning to Kim. He took a brief glance at the sleeping child. "She is cute...when she's not crying."

He sat next to Kim, turning sideways until he faced her. He stroked his fingertips across the back of her hand. "In case you couldn't guess—" he allowed a self-effacing chuckle "—I don't have any experience with kids."

She joined in with his laugh, the moment surprisingly light and open considering how strained things had been when she saw him on Saturday. "Yes, I did get that impression."

The soft touch of his fingertips turned to a covering of her hand with his, then a lacing of their fingers together. He gently tugged at her hand, drawing her closer until their faces were almost touching. "I'm sorry about having to get you out in the middle of the night, but I sure appreciate your help." He brushed his lips against hers and lowered his voice to a whisper. "Thank you."

Jared folded her into his embrace and captured her mouth with a passion-filled kiss that spoke of much more than polite gratitude for her assistance. He twined his fingers in her hair. Once again the sensuality of this very sexy and dynamic man spoke to her most inner and primal level. His actions weren't aggressive or forceful in a negative manner, and she did not feel threatened or frightened in any way, at least not physically threatened. She did, however, have to admit that he frightened her emotionally. He filled her with confusion over what to do and how to react. She knew she loved him, but his behavior the morning after they'd made love was so odd that she didn't know how to respond. Was he playing games with her?

Her longing for his attentions was matched by her fear of letting go and allowing him to know her true feelings. He was the wrong man for her. All her life, she had been told that the Stevens family could not be trusted. She knew the town gossip about his womanizing ways. He represented everything she had been taught to stay away from. It was an impossible situation. She had to put a stop to what was happening and make sure he knew that what had already happened was not to be repeated. She could not allow any more of his subtle and not-so-subtle advances to...

He pulled her body tighter against his, and despite her staunch intentions she melted in his embrace. Her arms seemed to have a will of their own as they encircled his neck. He nibbled at the corners of her lips, then captured her mouth with a new intensity that took her breath away. Memories of their passionate lovemaking filled her with an aching desire for more.

A moment later a surge of panic swept through Kim, telling her how close she had been to succumbing once again to his all too tempting seduction, that she wanted what was happening as much as he did. She pulled back from him, breaking off the kiss, but he continued to hold her in his embrace.

"Jared, stop." She fought to bring her ragged breathing under control. "This is very wrong."

"Wrong?" His labored breathing matched hers. He traced her kiss-swollen lips with the tip of his finger, sending another wave of desire through her body. "Why would you think this is wrong? It wasn't wrong the other night and it isn't wrong now.''

The disappointment in his eyes reached out to her as strongly as the magnetic pull of his sexual energy. She didn't know how to answer his question. It was wrong because they shouldn't be doing it. It was wrong because she loved him and he didn't return that love. It was wrong because he had dismissed her from his bed after they had made love.

Was this the way he treated all his women? Did he consider every woman who crossed his path fair game for his bedroom antics? Or was the man who had been terrified of the crying child yet continued to show such deep concern about her care, more akin to the real Jared Stevens? She knew the charming, outgoing Jared Stevens, but was that the real Jared? Everything about him bewildered her and left her feeling very confused.

She forced her attention to the sleeping child as she eased her way out of the warmth of his arms. She tried to divert his attention to more immediate and important matters. ''You never told me how Chloe got here.'' She scooted a few inches down the sofa to put a little space between them.

Jared kept hold of Kim's hand, refusing to relinquish the warmth he found so appealing and comforting. He knew this was not the time for him to pursue another physical encounter with her, but there was something about her that sent his common sense out of the room. He was left to wrestle with the desire coursing through his body every time he thought about her, every time he pulled up the vivid memory of the night they made love.

He stretched his long legs out in front of him and leaned his head back as he laced his fingers with hers. He furrowed his brow in concentration for a moment before relating the information about the little girl.

"Chloe...she was a total surprise to me. What I gather from Terry's hurried comments is that he got a girl pregnant and about eighteen months ago she had the baby. I have no idea who the mother is or what contact Terry had with her between then and now. This evening she dumped Chloe on Terry saying she couldn't care for her, so the little girl was now his responsibility. Terry showed up here with Chloe about midnight. He admitted he was the father but said he wasn't cut out to raise any children. Typical of Terry, he decided it wasn't his problem, either. He handed me the child, dropped the duffel bag on the floor and announced he was going on vacation."

Jared allowed a sigh of resignation that held an equal amount of weariness. "The last I saw of Terry was his taillights disappearing down the driveway. Three hours later I called you. Now you know as much about this as I do."

"What do you plan to do? You don't have any idea who the mother is or how to contact her?"

"Not a clue. If Terry hadn't admitted paternity, I wouldn't have believed it. It's the only time in his life he didn't immediately come looking for money so he could buy his way out of a scrape. How and why he managed to keep this a secret until now is beyond me. I can only surmise that he knew I'd never let him have the money to buy his way out of this rather than accept his responsibility."

It had been a telling statement, hearing Jared talking about Terry, knowing Jared would insist he accept responsibility for his actions. It was certainly not the type of sentiment she would have expected from the irresponsible playboy everyone thought Jared was.

"What do you plan to do with Chloe? Are you going to start a search for her mother?"

"I'll put Grant Collins on it in the morning. Meanwhile,

she'll stay here until I'm satisfied that she has someplace safe to go.''

"Don't you think you should call the authorities? After all, she's an abandoned child.''

"No! I'm not calling the police or child welfare.''

"But how are you going to take care of her? Look what happened tonight. I really think you should call the police.''

Jared abruptly let go of her hand and leaped to his feet. "No! No police. I'm not going to have her shuffled around more than she already has been.'' He headed toward the door.

She jumped up and started after him. "Wait a minute. It's not that easy. You can't just keep her here. There are laws—''

"No!'' He turned and glared at her. "No police, and that's final.''

"It's not final. This is an abandoned child. You have to notify the authorities. If you don't, you might be accused of kidnapping or something like that.''

"Chloe was not abandoned.'' Jared's words were emphatic and his expression determined. "She was left with me, a responsible adult who also happens to be a relative. After all, her father is my brother…half brother actually, but that still makes me her uncle.''

"But—''

"There is no but and there will be no police or child welfare services.'' He softened his tone as he walked across the room toward Kim. "Look, she'll be okay. I'll contact Grant first thing in the morning—'' he glanced at his watch "—make that later this morning, and I'll have him start an inquiry about the identity and location of the mother. He'll probably put a private detective on it.''

He took her hand in his and gave it a reassuring squeeze that said everything would be all right. This was an entirely different Jared Stevens than her preconceived notions and personal experience had presented to her. This was a caring and concerned man trying to do the right thing for a child rather than thinking only about himself and his comfort. It was a very appealing new facet to what she already knew was a sexy and desirable man.

"In the meantime, I'll access Terry's financial records and see if he's been paying money to anyone on a regular basis." A sarcastic chuckle escaped his throat. "Other than his bookie, of course. Or it might have been a lump sum payment eighteen months ago, or even earlier than that, perhaps when this woman informed him she was pregnant with his child. He might have paid her off then, assuming she would get an abortion and the problem would be over."

He tugged on Kim's hand as he edged his way toward the door. "Come to the kitchen with me. It's daylight out. There's no point in you going home now. Let's have some breakfast."

Kim glanced at the sleeping child. "We can't leave Chloe here. If she wakes up, she'll be all alone and she won't know where she is. She'll be scared."

"She's sound asleep. Besides, she spent most of the night awake and crying. She's probably exhausted and won't wake up for a while. We can bring our breakfast in here if you're worried."

She hesitated for a moment. "Well, I guess it will be okay. You're right, she's most likely exhausted."

"We won't be gone that long."

He gently tugged on her hand until she started walking. He continued to hold her hand as they went to the kitchen. What he really wanted was for her to be in his arms, but he would have to settle for the warmth created by their clasped hands for the time being. She had told him their being together was wrong, but he didn't know why she thought so. It all felt very right to him. He had never made love with a woman who felt more right.

It wasn't about a notch on his bedpost or another conquest. It was about something very different, something he still didn't want to identify, even though he had tentatively put a name to it…love. It was a puzzlement, and every time he thought about it he ended up with an uneasy sensation that kept poking at him, and as much as he hated to admit it, he knew why—the idea scared him. He had never been in love before. He wasn't even sure what it meant.

As soon as Jared turned on the kitchen light, Lurch barked from the utility room. Kim opened the door. Lurch charged into the room, tried to stop and ended up sliding across the floor. He threw himself into the situation by jumping up on Jared and happily greeting him with a sloppy kiss as Jared scratched behind his ears.

"Good morning, Lurch. This is a little early for you. Do you want your breakfast now, too?" Lurch gave an enthusiastic bark, then turned his attention to Kim. He lumbered over to her but didn't jump up on her.

Kim bent down and stroked the Saint Bernard's large head, then glanced at Jared. "Let me guess. Would I mind feeding the dog while you make coffee? Is that close?"

The devilishly sexy smile she had seen often enough to know its effect on her lit up his face. "I think you've finally caught on to how it works."

She shook her head as she tried unsuccessfully to suppress a grin. She had decided to accept her dog chores as not intentionally being anything demeaning or inconsequential he had dumped on her. He obviously was very close to Lurch and thought the dog's needs were important. Besides, she had grown very fond of the large, cumbersome Saint Bernard since that morning he had knocked her to the floor. "Come on, Lurch. Let's get your breakfast."

She set out the dog's food. When she returned to the kitchen Jared thrust a mug of hot coffee in her hands, then opened the refrigerator door and stared at the contents. He stifled a yawn as he reached for the orange juice. "You didn't make it back for breakfast Saturday morning, so let's try again."

Lurch let out a bark as the sound of someone entering the house reached their ears. A moment later Fred Kemper appeared at the kitchen door, having taken his usual way into the main house from the apartment above the garage where he lived. The look of surprise on his face said it all—seeing Kim and Jared fixing breakfast at that hour of the morning was the last thing he expected to encounter.

"You folks are sure up mighty early this mornin'."

Jared stole a furtive glance at Kim, which only increased her discomfort over Fred's choice of words and their implications. Did he really think she had spent the night with Jared? Was it that common for Fred to find a woman in the house so early?

"Good morning, Fred." Jared's voice was upbeat. He didn't show any signs of awkwardness over the situation. "We've had an interesting emergency. Kim was nice enough to come over a couple of hours ago when I called and begged her for help."

A warm feeling settled inside her. Without missing a beat Jared had dispelled any erroneous thoughts Fred might have had about her presence at that hour of the morning and had done it without any embarrassment to her. It was the same type of protective feeling she had gotten when he had put a stop to Terry's verbal abuse. But it was not at all the same feeling she had gotten from him when she woke up in his bed on Saturday morning.

"Oh? What kind of emergency you talkin' about? You

should of given me a shout instead of gettin' Kim out in the middle of the night.''

''I normally would have—'' Lurch bumped against Jared, nearly knocking him off balance as the dog charged out of the kitchen.

Jared watched as the large Saint Bernard disappeared down the hall, then returned his attention to Fred. ''As I was saying, I normally would have called you, but I think this one was a little out of your realm of expertise. We now have a houseguest who will be staying with us for an indefinite period of time.''

''Oh? Someone from out of town?''

Jared furrowed his brow in concentration. ''I really don't know, but I imagine she probably is.''

Fred cocked his head, a questioning look on his face, but when Jared didn't elaborate he chose to pour himself a cup of coffee rather than pursuing the conversation.

Kim started toward the door carrying her mug of coffee. ''I think I'll check on Chloe. I'm worried about her rolling off the sofa.''

''Wait.'' Jared started after her. ''I'll go with you.''

Kim heard Fred's voice as she headed toward the den. ''Since no one seems willin' to tell me what's goin' on, I'll just be fixin' us some breakfast.''

Kim and Jared came to an abrupt halt as soon as they entered the den. Lurch stood next to the sofa with his body against the edge. Chloe was still sleeping. She had apparently rolled over, and Lurch had prevented her from falling off by using his body as a barrier. The dog looked at them as if asking for their help.

Kim rushed over and gently moved the little girl to the middle of the sofa. As soon as physical contact was removed from the dog, Lurch sat down and sniffed at the child.

Jared affectionately stroked the dog's head and gave him a hug. "Good boy, Lurch. This is Chloe, and she's going to be staying with us for a while. Do you suppose you could help look out for her?"

To Kim's amazement the Saint Bernard gave up a quiet bark as if he understood Jared's words.

She turned her attention to Jared. "You really need to get a crib for her or some type of a bed with sides on it so there won't be any danger of her falling out of bed while she sleeps. I'm sure you can rent one for a day or so. And there's more than just a bed. With a toddler in the house you'll need to childproof so many things. At eighteen months she's walking everywhere and is more than capable of getting into anything within her reach. You need to make sure that cupboard doors can't be opened or drawers pulled out. Things sitting around on coffee tables or end tables need to be put up higher. Anything she can put in her mouth and choke on has to be moved out of her reach. And the swimming pool…you'll need to be very careful with the doors. If she can get onto the deck, then she can easily fall into the swimming pool or the hot tub."

Kim glanced around the attractively decorated den. "Having a toddler in the house is going to wreck havoc with your interior decor, especially that gorgeous living room and dining room."

Jared stood next to her and put his arm around her shoulder. He watched the little girl for a couple of moments as she slept. "Does this mean that you've decided I'm right about her staying here until we can sort this thing out?"

His words caught her by surprise. "No—I mean…well, maybe it wouldn't hurt for a day or so—at least until your attorney has an opportunity to check on the identity of her mother."

"Good. I'm glad that's settled." His arm felt good

around her shoulder. There was something comfortable about the two of them standing there watching the sleeping child. It filled her with a sense of contentment, a warm sensation that left her wondering what it would be like to have this man as a permanent part of her life, to have a family of her own.

"Breakfast is on." Fred's voice broke into the quiet moment.

"Shall we?" Jared took her hand. "We'll bring our food in here." He turned his attention to the dog. "Lurch, you stay here with Chloe. We'll be right back."

Eight

Kim set the large shopping bags on the desk, then went to the car and brought in more of her purchases. She removed the items from the sacks…disposable diapers, clothing, a few toys and a couple of children's books. She went to the car for a third time to bring in the box containing a stroller. When she returned from her fourth trip carrying the toddler car seat, she encountered Jared. Lurch was next to him, with Chloe sitting on the dog's back as if she was riding a pony. The little girl's laugh lit up her face and sent a wave of relief through Kim. Her concerns about leaving Chloe with Jared were apparently unfounded.

Kim looked quizzically at Jared. "How did you get your dog to act the part of a toddler-size horse?"

"It didn't take any work on my part. The two of them seem to have a natural affinity for each other. Lurch is curious about this little person and has become protective of her. I think it started when he kept her from rolling off the sofa while she was sleeping.''

"How did you and Chloe get along while I was gone?" She couldn't hide the wariness in her voice. She had been reluctant to leave the little girl alone with Jared while she did the shopping, but he had insisted that she was better qualified to make the purchases than he was, and obviously it had worked out all right. "Did she give you any trouble?"

Jared ignored her questions as he helped her unpack the bags. "You look like you have enough stuff here to last for weeks."

"Not really. You'd be surprised at how quickly a toddler can go through things." She handed him his credit card and the receipts for the purchases. "How is Fred coming with his childproofing chores?"

"He's about done. Child-proof fasteners on all the low cupboards and the drawers, gates at both the top and bottom of the staircase, covers on the electrical outlets. I've taken everything small and breakable off the coffee tables and end tables. The pool has an automatic roll-on cover that I'll keep closed when the pool's not in use. The hot tub is always covered when not in use. I called and am having a crib delivered. It should be here any time. I also made sure she had her midmorning snack just like you instructed. Now, is there anything else we need to do?"

She stopped unpacking and fixed him with a level gaze. "Do you mean other than calling the authorities about an abandoned child?"

His expression became stern. "We've already been through this. No police and no child welfare people. She stays here with me, at least until we can get this thing sorted out and find her mother."

Jared softened his manner as he reached out and gently

touched Kim's cheek. "You look tired. I think you should go home and get some sleep. Fred and I can manage here."

"Oh?" She gave him a dubious look. "Like you managed to change her diaper and handle her crying last night?"

"But now I know what to do and how to do it."

"Sure you do." Her skepticism came through loud and clear.

"You don't sound convinced."

She handed him the box containing the stroller. "It says here some assembly required. Do you think you can handle that?"

He took the box from her. "No problem."

Kim took Chloe off the dog's back. She smiled at the little girl and gave her a kiss on the cheek. "And you can come with me. We're going to take a bath and then put on some nice new clothes."

Jared set the box on the desk and turned his attention to Kim. "Did I hear that correctly?" A lascivious grin spread across his face, matching the lustful gleam in his eyes. "*We* are going to take a bath? You and Chloe in the tub together? Do you need any help? Can I wash your back? And if not, can I at least watch?"

She shot him a disdainful glare, then took the little girl's hand. "Come on, Chloe. Jared has work to do." Lurch trailed along behind them as they left the office reception room.

Jared watched them for a moment as they walked away. It was a sight that grabbed his senses and refused to let go. It was a family portrait of togetherness and contentment, of a mother and child engaged in the simple joys of everyday life. He found it strangely appealing and at the same time uncomfortably disturbing. He turned his attention to assembling the stroller, but he couldn't shake the image of Kim and Chloe from his mind.

He worked quickly and efficiently. When he had finished with the stroller he unpacked the car seat and inspected it. He sat on the edge of the desk and took a good look at the many items Kim had purchased for Chloe. He had been a little nervous about taking care of Chloe by himself while she was gone, but he had been right in insisting that Kim do the shopping. He picked up one of the books. It never would have occurred to him to buy a book to read to the little girl. And the disposable diapers…he had no idea they came in various sizes. That would have stumped him, too.

He really did not know the first thing about children. He wouldn't have thought about the things that needed to be done to childproof a house, either. He would have managed to get breakable items moved to higher places, but the need for safety fasteners on cupboards and drawers and electrical outlets never would have entered his mind. It had been very fortunate that Kim had been available to help him get organized. He knew he somehow would have managed without her, but it would have been a matter of trial and error, with lots of uneasy moments along the way.

And the time while Kim was gone…well, he had no idea that toddlers could move so fast. It took a constant vigil on his part to keep up with her while trying to childproof the house. With luck she would slow down after satisfying her curiosity by exploring and inspecting her new surroundings. He tried to stifle a yawn without any success. He had already been exhausted from being up all night without the added element of running after an active child all morning. He allowed a soft chuckle. He was only thirty-eight, but for a moment he felt closer to fifty.

The ringing doorbell interrupted his thoughts. A minute later there was a crib standing in his entryway. He took it upstairs and rolled it down the hallway toward his bedroom, not sure exactly where he was going to put it. He stopped in front of the guest bedroom across the hall from his room. The sounds of Chloe laughing filtered into the hallway. He pushed the crib into the guest bedroom, then peeked into the private bathroom on the other side of the room.

Kim was on her knees leaning across the edge of the bathtub. Chloe had splashed water all over the front of Kim's T-shirt. His gaze focused on the way the wet fabric clung to her breasts. A tightness pulled across his chest, and an apprehensive jitter flitted around inside his stomach. His mind went to the lovemaking they had shared, to the earthy sensuality of their togetherness.

He watched her with Chloe a few minutes longer. A surprising sensation of warmth spread through his body. Unlike what his life had been before, Kim's presence left him feeling somehow settled and content. He didn't know where the feeling came from or why it was there, but it felt good. Then a sharp jab of panic overpowered the contentment and sent a nervous tremor through his consciousness.

"How are you getting along in here?" He didn't like the slightly husky sound of his voice.

A startled Kim looked up. "I didn't hear you come in." She returned to rinsing the shampoo from Chloe's hair as she spoke. "We're just about done. Normally she wouldn't take a bath in the middle of the day, but I don't know when she last had one. I'll put her pajamas on her, feed her lunch, then put her down for a much needed nap. I'm surprised she's not cranky after the disturbed night she had."

"The crib is here. I thought I'd put it in my bedroom so she wouldn't feel alone at night, and that way I would hear her if she woke up and wanted something."

Kim lifted the little girl out of the bathtub and wrapped her in a large bath towel. She had been thinking about where to put the crib when it arrived, but wasn't sure how to express her reservations about what he had decided.

"Are you sure that's what you want to do?" She busied herself drying Chloe. It provided her with an excuse for not looking at him as she said what was on her mind. "I mean...it would be very intrusive into your personal life. You'd run the risk of waking her when you got ready for bed at night or when you got up in the morning." Kim towel dried Chloe's hair, then combed it. "It's just that since you insist on keeping her here for a day or so, I think it might be better if she had her own room."

Kim dressed the little girl while Jared moved the crib into place. She stood holding the toddler's hand. "I think we're ready to go to the kitchen and have lunch now."

Jared started off at a quick pace, then stopped and turned to wait for Kim and Chloe to catch up with him. A sheepish expression covered his features as he gestured toward the little girl. "The way she ran around while you were out shopping, I just assumed she'd walk that fast, too."

"She has little legs and can only take little steps."

The three of them proceeded to the kitchen, where Fred was putting away his tools.

"I've finished here, Jared. If that's all you need, I'd best be gettin' myself downtown to the construction site. I should've been there three hours ago."

"You go ahead. Thanks, Fred, for taking care of this for me."

Kim watched as Fred exited through the utility room then turned toward Jared. "A construction project?"

"It's nothing." Jared looked around as if searching for something. "Anything special you want for lunch? What about Chloe? What can we fix for her?"

Kim immediately recognized Jared's attempt to change the topic. What was he trying to hide? Well, Otter Crest wasn't that large. A new construction project should be easy to spot. Maybe he wasn't going to answer her question, but she fully intended to take a detour in that direction on her way home.

She stifled a yawn. She had only been asleep about four hours when Jared called her at three o'clock that morning and she had been going nonstop ever since. She stifled another yawn as she reached for the refrigerator door. He reached out and grasped her hand as he stared into the depths of her blue eyes.

Jared continued to clutch her hand, not wanting to let go of the warmth that radiated to his senses. Every time he touched her he wanted to carry her off to his bedroom and make love to her. And there was more. He wanted more, but exactly what it was that he wanted frightened him to the point where he refused to acknowledge it. He tugged on her hand, pulling her closer to him.

"Hungry." A little hand yanked at the bottom of Kim's T-shirt, breaking what could have easily become an intimate moment of seduction that she knew she needed to avoid. She eased her hand out of his. Equal parts of relief and disappointment assailed her senses as she broke the physical contact.

Kim stirred as the sleep lifted from her brain, then she suddenly sat upright. She pulled back the bedspread that covered her. She furrowed her brow in confusion. She didn't recall having pulled the spread over her. She checked the time and was surprised to find that she had been sleeping for two hours. She remembered putting Chloe down for her nap following lunch, then stretching out on the bed in the guest room. *Just until Chloe gets to sleep,* she had thought. She knew she was tired but had no idea she was so tired that she would fall asleep as soon as her head hit the pillow.

She glanced toward the crib to check on Chloe and spotted Jared. He was asleep in a large easy chair he had pulled next to the crib. He had to be even more exhausted than she was. At least she had gotten about four hours of sleep before his call woke her. He hadn't had any sleep at all.

She stared at his handsome features. Even though he was sleeping, the expression on his face gave him an uneasy look beyond the understandable exhaustion, as if something was troubling him. He had taken a great deal of responsibility on himself when he had decided to keep Chloe at his house. And he had done it without consideration for what was in it for him. His every spoken concern had been for the little girl's welfare rather than his convenience. It was a very admirable and selfless decision for someone she had originally pegged as nothing more than an irresponsible playboy.

She looked at the bedspread and the way it had been pulled from the other side of the bed so it covered her. Had Jared done that? Had he acted on a genuine concern for her comfort with the personal gesture of covering her? A warm feeling spread through her body. His actions were totally out of character for the person she had assumed Jared Stevens was, especially after the tension that filled the air the morning after they had made love. Her assumptions were melting quicker than a block of ice in the desert sun.

There was nothing about Jared that fit in with her preconceived notions before they made love, and not after they had made love, either. She had been off balance where he was concerned from the moment he first walked through the door of her father's house. And during the ensuing month he had kept her off balance by constantly doing and saying unexpected things. She glanced at the bedspread he had pulled over her body as she slept, then at the way he had moved his chair next to the crib in a protective manner. Those were not the actions of a selfish, arrogant man whose only purpose was to belittle and humiliate others in a desire to make himself feel superior—not the type of attitude or treatment she had always received from Terry.

Those were the actions of the man she had fallen in love with, a man who had a lot to offer to the world, a man who wasn't afraid of responsibility. As much as she didn't want to admit it, she had no other choice than to allow her thoughts and emotions free rein. She had initially fought the notion that she was falling in love with him, but she could no longer deny the existence of that very real love. If only she could understand the odd change in his attitude Saturday morning after they woke. There must have been something she missed, some indication of what had happened. Was it possible she had said or done something to cause his strange behavior?

She slid off the bed and quietly approached the crib. A little eighteen-month-old toddler dumped on him in the middle of the night, and his immediate course of action was to accept full responsibility for taking care of her and trying to find her mother. The admiration she felt for him welled inside her. Perhaps her love had not been misplaced, after all.

Jared stirred, then sat bolt upright. He stretched his arms above his head as he stood. He glanced at Chloe before turning his attention to Kim. The sheepish expression on his face told of his embarrassment. "I guess we all needed a little nap. Hopefully things can now get on some sort of schedule so we can get some work done around here."

"Yes, it has been a lost day." She adjusted Chloe's blanket. "She seems to have adapted to her new surroundings very quickly." A moment of sadness claimed her before she was able to shake it off. "Did she ask for her mother while I was shopping this morning?"

"No." He frowned as he considered her question. "I expected her to, but she didn't. She seemed content to look around, explore the house and bask in Lurch's attentions."

"I'm surprised at the way Lurch and Chloe seem to be bonding. I would have thought a dog that size would have been frightening for such a little tyke."

Jared laughed. "Lurch is just a big, overgrown puppy. He loves everyone. Not exactly prime qualities for a watch-dog." He glanced at the sleeping child again, a slight frown telling of his apprehension. "Do you need to wake her up? If she sleeps too long, will she be awake all night again?"

"I don't think so. She should wake up on her own pretty soon."

He shook his head as he expelled a sigh of resignation. "I had no idea there was so much to consider when having a toddler in the house." He reached out, lightly stroked his fingertips across Kim's cheek, then took her hand in his.

Jared plumbed the depths of her eyes looking for...looking for what? Did she dare hope it was something personal? An intimate question of sharing and togetherness? A sign that he cared deeply for her as more than just a lover?

His voice softened to a mere whisper yet carried a strength of character she had come to realize was an integral part of him. "Did I remember to thank you for coming to my rescue?"

The tender moment tugged at her heartstrings. She did not want to pursue any antagonism. Did she dare hope for a relationship built on more than a temporary contracted work arrangement and one night of passionate lovemaking? Was she again treading into dangerous territory with this forbidden man?

Chloe woke from her nap, interrupting the tender moment that seemed to be drawing Jared and Kim emotionally together while erasing the bad feelings from their morning-after confrontation. Kim allowed an inward sigh of relief that something had put a halt to her errant and inappropriate musings. She lifted the little girl out of the crib and gave her a hug.

"Did you have a good nap, Chloe?"

Chloe squirmed in Kim's arms, trying to get down as she looked around the room. "Doggy?"

As Kim set her on the floor, Lurch appeared from the hallway as if on cue. Kim held the teddy bear toward Chloe, but she ignored it. Instead of reaching for the toy, she laughed, got to her feet and rushed toward the large Saint Bernard.

Jared watched the interaction between Chloe and Lurch. It was a heartwarming sight. And equally touching had been Kim's response to the little girl and her willingness to help make the child feel welcome, safe and secure in spite of her stated objections to his decision not to call the police. It was a family feeling...at least what he assumed a family feeling would be like.

For most of his life the words *family* and *dysfunctional* had been pretty much synonymous. His mother and father had divorced when he was only five years old. His father had remarried a year later, and two years after that, Terry was born. His mother had died when he was twelve, which was when he had gone to live with his father and what was to be the first in a long line of stepmothers.

None of his stepmothers had been what he would call motherly, which certainly went a long way in explaining Terry's attitude toward life. And Ron Stevens had been so busy working his underhanded deals along with his legitimate business interests that he was more like a stranger who lived in the same house than a father.

It seemed all his life he had been searching for something, but he never knew what it was. He had tried to find it in myriad beds and casual affairs but found only physical satisfaction—never the emotional connection he had been looking for. Could family be that missing element he so desperately wanted to find?

His gaze drifted from Chloe to Kim. Could Kim Donaldson be the answer to his quandary? Not only was she a very desirable woman who sent his libido into overload, but once he had gotten beyond her hostile exterior he had discovered a caring and compassionate woman who pulled at his emotions as strongly as she did his sexual desires. Then they had made love. It had been the most profound awakening of his life, an awakening of his emotions and the opening of his heart. It had also been the most frightening experience of his life. Love. He wasn't even sure he knew what it meant, let alone what to do about it.

Kim turned her attentions from Lurch and Chloe to Jared. "Have you talked to your attorney about Chloe's mother?"

"Yes, I spoke to Grant Collins this morning while you were shopping. He'll put a private investigator on it right away. He didn't know anything about Chloe, either. Whatever Terry did about the fact that he had gotten this woman pregnant didn't involve our attorney. I'm still amazed that he managed to keep this a secret from everyone for so long."

Kim glanced at her watch. "I really should get some work done before the day is completely gone. I need to get started on calling the hotels and gathering price information—"

"Not today. You've already done more than enough. You've been here since about three-fifteen this morning.

Why don't you call it a day and go home. Of course—''
he took her hand in his ''—if you'd like to stay and have
dinner with Chloe and me that would be nice, too.'' He
flashed that sexy smile that never failed to melt whatever
resolve she had. ''I'm sure Chloe would appreciate it if you
stayed for dinner.''

And after dinner, then what? Kim's mind rushed to the
night they had made love, to the passion and excitement
that reinforced the love she felt for him. Did he have an
ulterior motive in asking her to stay for dinner? Was it her
own desires that had put the thought in her mind? She eyed
him suspiciously as she worked her hand out of his grasp
before she succumbed to any more of the subtle methods
of seduction he seemed to excel at.

''You're using a toddler to manipulate the circumstances? Isn't that just a wee bit unethical?''

''Using Chloe? Not at all. I just thought you'd want to
make sure I didn't do anything wrong between now and
her bedtime.''

She regarded him for a moment, trying to read his expression and body language in an attempt to figure out what
was really going on in his head. Were her natural suspicions
of a Stevens family member coloring her assessment of the
situation? She didn't know. She wanted to trust Jared, but
after what happened the morning following the night they'd
made love, she didn't know if she could. Would she ever
be able to put the specter of the Stevens–Donaldson feud
and all her father's beliefs and teachings behind her?

She hesitated a moment. ''Well…maybe until we get her
down to sleep.''

''Good, let's—''

''But between now and then I'll take Chloe with me to
the office area so I can get some work done while keeping
an eye on her.''

He took her hand again. "I suppose you're right. I have lots to do, and today has been a total loss as far as work is concerned."

She cocked her head and furrowed her brow in concentration for a moment. "That little conference room between the reception area and your office…do you use it very often?"

"No, not really. Why?"

"I think it would make a good playroom for Chloe, somewhere close to the office where we could keep an eye on her during the day and still be able to work."

He tugged on her hand, drawing her closer to him until their faces were almost touching. "That's a good idea." He brushed his lips against hers, then allowed his kiss to linger for a couple of seconds, once again sending her resolve into hiding. She finally managed to break away from his kiss.

He looked at her questioningly. "What do we need to do to turn it into a playroom?"

Kim stifled a yawn as she carried some preliminary estimates in to Jared for using ballrooms at various downtown hotels. She paused while passing through the newly converted playroom to talk to Chloe for a moment. The little girl seemed happy and content with her toys and Lurch's attention. A moment of sadness tinged her feelings as she thought about Chloe being abandoned by her mother and the strange situation of the toddler not even asking where her mother was or showing any signs of concern.

Chloe didn't appear to be afraid of her new surroundings or the strangers who were taking care of her. In fact, she seemed like such a happy child that it made the circumstances of her sudden arrival at Jared's house all the more strange. It was a puzzling situation and one that continued to leave Kim feeling uneasy about Jared's decision to attempt to find Chloe's mother rather than calling the authorities.

She left Chloe with her toys, carried the paperwork into Jared's office and set it on his desk. "This is what I've been able to put together so far on preliminary estimates. None of the hotels can give me any more than this without a head count. I don't know if we're talking about one hundred people or one thousand people."

She glanced at her watch. "I'll prepare Chloe's dinner, then I'd better get home before I fall asleep again." A warm feeling flowed through her veins as she recalled the way Jared had covered her, then pulled a chair next to the crib where he had fallen asleep. It was certainly not the type of considerate gesture she would have expected from a Stevens...at least, not before getting to know Jared the way she had. But how well did she really know him? The man responsible for that consideration was also the man who practically shooed her out the door after their night of lovemaking. He was as much of a puzzle now as he was before they'd made love.

Jared rose from his chair, took her hand and pulled her close to him. His voice may have carried a teasing quality, but his eyes showed his seriousness. "If you're tired, I can find a place for you to stay tonight. It will save you that long drive home."

Kim's heart pounded a little harder, and her breath came a little quicker. She was not a promiscuous woman and did not fall into bed with every handsome man who smiled at her. She didn't want to be just another one of Jared's conquests. Was it possible she could be someone different from the long string of women he had romanced over the years? Someone who might have a chance of winning his heart? She didn't want to dwell on those thoughts.

She was afraid to allow herself the possibility of believing she could be the one woman to capture his heart. As much as she thrilled to her night of lovemaking with Jared, she wished it had never happened. She feared it would only lead to heartbreak, rather than the lifetime of happiness she had envisioned.

She decided the best course of action was to go along with his teasing tone rather than the seriousness in his eyes—it was safer, emotionally safer. "Long drive? You mean that huge three-mile distance from here to my father's house?"

He pulled her closer, wrapping one arm around her waist while continuing to hold her hand. "Yep...that's the long drive I'm talking about."

It suddenly seemed as if all the oxygen had been sucked from the room and someone had turned the heat on. His nearness sent tremors of excitement through her body. She experienced a moment of light-headedness. She finally managed to force out some words while attempting to maintain a teasing persona. "I thank you for your kind offer, but I think it would be better for everyone concerned if I went home rather than staying here."

He nuzzled the side of her neck. "That's a matter of opinion. Better for whom?"

His hot breath grazed her cheek, then his lips pressed behind her ear. She swallowed hard as she fought to catch her breath and maintain her composure. There was no way she should be allowing this to happen, but she didn't want it to stop, either. "It's my opinion, and I'm the one who will be making that long drive." In the back of her mind, fighting its way through the sensual fog that engulfed her conscious thoughts, was the snippet of conversation she had heard that morning between Jared and Fred about the downtown construction project. She wanted to find out what it was and Jared's connection to it.

His words came out as a whisper. "You don't have to go home unless you really want to." His mouth found hers, knocking the speculations from her mind. The spine-tingling kiss grabbed her senses and refused to let go. She felt herself slipping under his magnetic spell. She wrapped her arms around his neck and returned the kiss. She already knew he was everything a woman could ask for as a lover, but she wanted more than that. Was Jared able to provide what she wanted out of life? Was he someone who could make a commitment to a relationship and stick to it? Was she the woman who would be able to obtain that commitment? She didn't know.

With her last remaining modicum of control she managed to break the delicious kiss and pull away from his all-too-tempting seduction. She gasped a few words. "I need to fix dinner for Chloe."

"Let's get some dinner for all of us—" he pulled her into his arms "—as soon as I finish this." He claimed her mouth, but this time he ended the kiss after only a few seconds. He took her hand and they walked to the newly converted playroom to get Chloe. The three of them continued to the kitchen.

Kim prepared Chloe's dinner while Jared put together some dinner for the adults. Again, he felt the closeness of family, the comfort and contentment of having Kim and Chloe with him. He knew it wasn't possible or feasible for Chloe to stay with him for long, that eventually the police would have to be called if the mother could not be found. His attorney had made that very clear to him. Even though he was the little girl's uncle and therefore a relative, due to the unusual circumstances it did not relieve him of the responsibility of reporting what had happened.

And Kim. She was only there because of a letter of agreement stating that she would work for the summer to pay off her father's debt. The warm sensation brought on by the family atmosphere of the current situation was a short-term deal. Did he want it to be more? To be permanent? The questions frightened him. He was not sure how he felt. He thought he loved her, but was it a true love? He'd never been in love before and wasn't sure he could properly recognize it. And if it was, then what was the next step? It scared him as much as it provided a surprising amount of comfort.

He had his long-held belief that commitment to a relationship wasn't worth the time it took to claim it existed. His father's many marriages, mistresses and affairs had shown him that. Was Kim the type of woman who would be agreeable to an affair, a no-strings-attached type of relationship? He didn't know, but everything about her said she would not consider such a proposition.

And what could he do if she didn't agree? The idea of Kim not being in his life was something he didn't want to consider.

Nine

After dinner, Kim dressed Chloe in her pajamas. She took the little girl's hand, and they walked to the kitchen where Jared was putting away the last of the dishes from the dishwasher.

She indicated the toddler. "I think we're ready for bed now."

She picked up Chloe and gave the little girl a kiss on the cheek. "Do you want to say good-night to your uncle Jared before you go to bed?"

Jared flashed his sexy smile at Kim. "It looks to me like only one of you is ready for bed."

She chose to ignore his pointed comment, twinkling eyes and killer smile, although it wasn't an easy task. "Do you want to say good-night to Chloe before I put her to bed?"

Jared took the little girl from Kim's arms and started talking to her as he carried her toward the stairs. Lurch trailed behind them, pausing every few steps to look back as if to make sure Kim was following them.

They reached the guest room, and Kim watched as Jared put the little girl in her crib. The contrast between the man whose face had been clearly etched with panic when she arrived after his frantic call and this man who took great care to tuck Chloe safely in her bed was startling. He seemed to take naturally to fatherhood. Could he adjust as easily to a committed relationship?

She walked to the edge of the crib and stood next to Jared, watching as the toddler yawned and fought to stay awake. It had been a busy day for her, filled with new people and new surroundings.

Jared put his arm around Kim's shoulder and drew her closer to him. "She isn't any trouble at all. Are all children this easy to care for?" He turned to face Kim, the expression on his face saying his question was sincere rather than facetious.

She could not stop her spontaneous laugh in response to his question. "Not even close. You've apparently forgotten your panicked phone call to me in the middle of the night when she wouldn't stop crying. I'll admit she seems to be a very happy child, but this isn't what I'd call the normal way things go with a toddler. This has been an exceptionally trouble-free day."

Chloe finally closed her eyes after a valiant attempt to stay awake. When it was obvious that she was asleep, Jared and Kim left the bedroom, taking Lurch with them.

"Well, I'd better get home. It's getting late."

Jared pulled her into his arms, and a moment later his lips were on hers. His kiss deepened, promising all the passion and excitement she had experienced in his bed. He broke the kiss just long enough to gasp out a few words.

"Come on…we'll have a glass of wine and then—"

"No, I really have to go home." She backed away from his embrace, thankful he had provided an opening that allowed her to recover her resolve. "I'll see you in the morning. I'll be here early so I can help with Chloe's breakfast."

With that Kim hurried out the door, got in her car and drove away. She tried to put the sexual magnetism of Jared Stevens out of her mind, but without much success. She attempted to concentrate on other things. She turned at the end of the block rather than continuing toward her father's house. As she approached downtown Otter Crest, she scanned the area for any new construction. She drove up and down several blocks until she came to the site of the new community center.

She took out a pad and pencil and copied all the information posted on the various signs...name of the construction company, name of the project under construction and name of the organization financing the community center. To her surprise it wasn't a bank. What she didn't find was the name Jared Stevens or Stevens Enterprises. She would check it out and see if she could find any connection between this building and Jared.

She had her eyes opened to a Jared Stevens she never would have believed existed, the type of person she had never associated with the Stevens family. He had taken her side against Terry's verbal abuse. He had apologized to her for Terry's rudeness. She had heard him say he believed some of his father's business dealings had been unethical and that those suspicions had left him uneasy. He also told her he had confidence in her ability to plan the charity event. And then, to top it all off, he had accepted full responsibility without reservation or hesitation for the care and safety of an eighteen-month-old girl he had never seen before...a responsibility that he took very seriously.

That was the Jared Stevens she had fallen in love with,

but was it the same Jared Stevens she would be seeing in the morning? The future was becoming more and more confusing. She emitted a little sigh of trepidation as she arrived home. She went straight to her bedroom, dropped her clothes in the middle of her bedroom floor, collapsed into bed and quickly dropped into an exhausted sleep.

Jared woke early. Somehow he had managed to sleep through the night while still keeping one ear attuned to any sounds from Chloe's room. He took a quick shower, dressed, then immediately checked on the little girl. She was still sleeping, her teddy bear clutched tightly in her arms.

He allowed his thoughts to drift over the previous few days, starting with the intensity and passion of the lovemaking he and Kim had shared. She was everything he wanted and everything he needed. She had given him a glimpse of what a real family could be like. It was an eye-opening revelation that belied his assumptions about relationships and family but didn't do anything to ease his deeply ingrained fears where commitment was concerned.

He went to the kitchen and made coffee. Kim said she would be at his house early to help with breakfast. He glanced at his watch and wondered how she defined early.

He didn't have to wonder for long. The doorbell rang, signaling her arrival. He opened the door and was immediately assailed by the warmth and sensuality of her presence.

"Good morning. I'm glad to see you."

An immediate look of concern flashed across her face. "Is something wrong? Is there a problem with Chloe? Why didn't you call me?" Without waiting for an answer Kim rushed toward the guest room with Jared right behind her.

"Wait…nothing's wrong. She's still asleep."

Kim came to a halt and eyed him questioningly. "Then why were you so glad to see me? I thought something was wrong."

He grasped her hand. "Does there have to be a problem? Can't I just be glad to see you?"

Confusion gripped her thoughts again. They had made love with an intensity that far exceeded anything she had ever before experienced. Then the next morning a definite tension materialized between them, a tension caused by Jared. She didn't understand why he had behaved the way he had, especially in light of his subsequent attentive behavior toward her.

A wave of irritation rippled through her. What kind of game was he playing? She took a couple of steps away from him as she eased her hand out of his, desperately needing to break the physical contact before she totally succumbed to his all-too-tempting touch.

"I don't know what's going on here, Jared, what you're trying to pull, but you're not going to sucker me into your web a second time. You know that old saying, 'fool me once, shame on you—fool me twice, shame on me.'" As soon as the words were out of her mouth she regretted them. She did not want to confront him about how she had been hurt by his casual dismissal of her from his bedroom as if she were a paid escort. She loved him, yet he had pulled back from her, and it hurt.

A look of total shock spread across his features, followed by bewilderment. "What are you talking about?"

She clenched her jaw as she turned away from him. "Never mind. It's nothing."

Jared grabbed her arm and whirled her around until she faced him. Flecks of anger sparked in his green eyes. "No, you don't. I'm not going to let you get away with that. I hate it when women pull that *it's nothing, never mind* routine. I don't know what you're talking about.''

She glared at him. ''Well, you should know.''

He continued to hold her arm in his strong grip, his gaze locking with hers in a battle of wills. ''But I don't know and I won't unless you tell me.''

Her confidence melted away quicker than she could stop it. She glanced at the floor, unable to maintain eye contact with him. *When am I ever going to learn to keep my mouth shut? Now he has me on the spot.* She had to share her thoughts, feelings and hurt with him or exacerbate the situation by telling him it was none of his business after she had already let him know it was something he had done.

His voice softened a little. ''Come on, Kim. Talk to me. I don't like playing games.''

Her head snapped up, her gaze once again locking with his in a brief battle of wills. ''You don't like playing games? What do you call that little number you pulled on me Saturday morning?'' Her anger returned full force, combined with the hurt she couldn't keep out of her voice. ''You handed me my clothes and as much as said I was dismissed. You practically shoved me out of your bed as if you couldn't get rid of me fast enough.''

A sharp stab of guilt shot through him. Her words were the last thing he had expected to hear. He knew he hadn't behaved in a very good manner, but he certainly hadn't intended it to be like that. He had been so confused that morning, unsure exactly where things stood and what was happening. He had felt trapped, as if the walls were closing in on him. But playing a game? That had definitely not been his intention. The very last thing he wanted was to have her think he was toying with her.

He pulled her into his arms and brushed a tender kiss against her lips. His voice was soft, containing the emotion that coursed through his veins. "I wasn't playing a game with you. I didn't mean for anything I said or did to make you feel that way. It's just that…"

He turned her loose, rubbed his hand across the back of his neck and nervously shifted his weight from one foot to the other. He didn't know what to say without exposing his true inner turmoil and the vulnerability he had tried so hard to keep hidden. But he knew he had to say something, offer some kind of explanation.

He placed his hands on her shoulders. "Kim…" He saw the uncertainty in her eyes and felt the tension in her muscles. He had to find the right words to ease her hurt without exposing his carefully guarded fears. He pulled her into his embrace, cradled her head against his shoulder and stroked her hair. If only he wasn't so afraid to say what was in his heart.

"I'm sorry, Kim. It was thoughtless on my part. It didn't occur to me that you would interpret bringing your clothes to the bedroom as my desire for you to leave. Quite the contrary. My only thought was that you might be uncomfortable without a robe or something to put on. I should have found something in my closet for you to wear."

He placed a gentle kiss against her forehead and continued to hold her in his arms. Had he said enough to soothe her concerns and allay her fears? He didn't know.

Kim wasn't sure how to reply to what he had said, but knew she had to say something. "Well…it was very upsetting for me."

"I'm sorry. If you'd mentioned it to me at the time, then we could have straightened out the misunderstanding right away instead of having it grow into this. Next time you have a problem with something I've said or done, promise me you'll let me know before it gets blown all out of proportion like this did…okay?"

He sounded so sincere, so honest. Did she dare trust that he really meant it? That the entire incident had been nothing more than a miscommunication? Possibly her anxiety and fears affecting her thoughts?

Her words came out barely above a whisper. "Okay, I'll mention it." As long as she remained in the warmth of his embrace she was like putty in his hands, ready to be molded into whatever he wanted. She had something else on her mind, too, and this would be a good time to mention it, to get it out into the open.

"I drove by the downtown construction site on my way home last night. The sign says it's going to be a community center. There's no mention of Stevens Enterprises, yet Fred Kemper is involved with it somehow. Is there a connection between you and the nonprofit organization listed on the sign?"

Jared paused as he gathered his thoughts. Her question had come out of left field, and he wasn't sure what to say. He didn't like to talk about the things he did through his nonprofit organization. He carefully measured his words.

"That organization is a part of Stevens Enterprises. It was something I started after taking over the company from my father. I use it for community projects where I see a need and for charity projects when I want the origin of the help to remain anonymous."

She didn't know what she had expected him to say, but that hadn't been it. She turned his words over in her mind before saying anything else. "Why didn't you tell me instead of avoiding the issue when I asked about Fred going to a construction site?"

"I didn't know it was an issue." A shiver of uncertainty made its way through his body. Jared had never been as on edge in his entire life as he had since he and Kim made love. It told him what he didn't want to know, what he had feared. It told him he might be in love with her. He mentally shook his head. There was no *might* about it. He was in love with her. And he had done everything wrong from the moment he had realized it.

He pulled her into his embrace. He didn't want to dwell on troubling matters. His words were tentative, and he wasn't sure exactly where he was going with them. "This is a very large house with five guest rooms. There's lots of space for you here." He shoved away the quick rush of anxiety. "I'm sure Chloe will be glad to have you around." He brushed a tender kiss against her lips. His voice dropped to a soft, intimate whisper. "And so will I."

As much as his words about her temporarily moving into his house excited her, he hadn't mentioned a word about commitment or love. Things were becoming very confused. She felt torn apart, her desires pulling her one way and reality tugging her in a different direction. Kim stepped back from the enticing warmth of his embrace. She had to keep her emotions out of this.

"I have something else I'd like to know, something that's on my mind—something else I hope you can clear up for me."

A ripple of anxiety assailed his senses. "What is it?"

"I want to know what you're looking for, Jared. A summer fling? A mistress of the month? A short-term affair? What is it you want from me? I'm tired of trying to guess." She looked into the depths of his green eyes. She didn't see any deception, but she didn't see any answers, either.

"I want to put the sins of the past behind us. I want to put this stupid family feud to rest once and for all." He paused as he tried to put his thoughts into words, but he couldn't seem to get them to jell into anything cohesive. He pulled her into his arms. "I want to enjoy the company of a beautiful and very desirable woman I think a great deal of and am so glad I had the opportunity to meet.''

The fear had once again claimed him. He had stopped short of telling her how he felt, telling her of his love— telling her he wanted them to have a future together that would last a lifetime. No matter how much he wanted to share those feelings with her, each time he tried to say the words they choked off in his throat.

A wave of disappointment crashed through Kim. She had asked for a commitment, some mention of his feelings toward her, and all she had received was pretty words. Could she live with the situation the way it was? An affair without a commitment? She wasn't sure how to respond to what he had said, so she said nothing.

She remained enfolded in his arms. If this was all there ever would be, could she afford to let it slip through her fingers because she wanted more? Would it serve any purpose to dwell on the fact that she couldn't have it all when she already had so much? She turned the thought over in her mind, but a moment later her entire reality was consumed by the heat of Jared's mouth on hers.

All Kim's worries and concerns vanished in a burst of heated desire. Jared Stevens was everything she wanted. She returned his kiss, reveling in the texture of his tongue against hers. Tremors of delight rippled across her skin in response to his touch. Being in his embrace felt so right. She wrapped her arms around his neck and totally gave herself up to his tender ministrations.

Jared scooped her up in his arms and carried her toward the stairs. She closed her eyes and allowed the anticipation to sweep over her senses, the sweet anticipation of what she knew would be the same intense lovemaking they had shared before—a combining of body and soul that told her how much she loved him.

As he passed the guest room door across from his bedroom, he suddenly came to a halt. One breathless whisper escaped his throat before he put Kim down.

"Chloe…"

Jared walked quietly into the guest room and peered into the crib. The little girl was sound asleep, her teddy bear clutched in her arm. She looked so peaceful, as if she didn't have a care in the world. A moment later Kim stood at his side. He put his arm around her shoulder and pulled her close.

The feeling of family closeness assailed his consciousness again, the same warm feeling he had experienced other times when he was with Kim and Chloe. It was a feeling of settled contentment, something that had never been part of his life before meeting Kim. He liked the way it felt.

He kissed Kim on the cheek before pulling her fully into his arms. "She looks like she's sound asleep. What do you think?" He nuzzled her neck and kissed the tender spot behind her ear.

Her words came out in a husky whisper. "She looks like she's sound asleep to me, too."

He took Kim's hand and together they walked into his bedroom. It took only a minute for them to divest themselves of their clothes and snuggle into the softness of the king-size bed.

The excitement raced through her veins. All her doubts and concerns about where her relationship with Jared Stevens was going vanished from her mind the moment his mouth came down on hers. The heated sparks of a few minutes earlier ignited with a passion that consumed everything in its path.

The sensation of their bare skin touching along the length of their torsos pushed her fervor to a new plane. Every nerve ending tingled with the ardor coursing through her body. She reached for his hardened manhood at the same time as his mouth found her tautly puckered nipple. She felt the shudder of his quick intake of breath when her fingers wrapped around his rigidity. A tangle of arms and legs, a meshing of bodies and the sounds of ragged breathing eclipsed anything and everything else.

Jared's fingers slid seductively up her inner thigh until he found her moist heat. Her moan of pleasure was swallowed up when his mouth again captured hers with a demanding intensity. He rolled her body on top of him as his fingers danced across the curve of her bottom. He wrapped his arms around her, holding her tightly against his body. His words came out in a breathless whisper. "Kim…Kim…you are so…I…"

He managed to stop his words just in time by burying his face in her hair, nuzzling her neck, then exploring the dark recesses of her mouth with his tongue. He had come so close to saying he loved her before his total fear of that final step overshadowed his innermost desires. He reached for the drawer of the nightstand and removed the packet.

Kim felt his labored breathing beneath her, the ragged rise and fall of his chest. She straddled his hips. His strong hands lifted, then lowered her onto his hardened manhood. A potent rush of sensual delight charged through her body, electrifying every sense receptor.

They moved in harmonic unity, so totally attuned to each other's needs that it was as if they had been making love together for years.

Kim arched her back and gasped as the waves of euphoria crashed through her body. She fell forward against his heaving chest, sated by the pleasure of the most dynamic man she had ever known.

Her mouth found his. He hungrily devoured her taste as he wrapped her securely in his embrace. He gave one final hard upward thrust followed by a deep growl of orgasmic rapture. He held her hips pressed tightly against his as he savored each spasm of release. No one set his soul on fire the way she did, and no one else would ever touch his heart with the love he felt for her. If only he could find a way to get past his fears so he could tell her of that love. He brushed a loose tendril of her hair away from her damp cheek, placed a tender kiss on her lips, then caressed her shoulders. He didn't want to ever let go of her.

Jared's breathing slowly returned to normal, as did Kim's. He nestled her head against his shoulder and stroked her hair. Neither of them spoke, each content to bask in the warm afterglow of their lovemaking.

Several thoughts ran through his mind—thoughts of love, of family and of the future. He wanted them to be together. He wanted to share his life with her. He had also been giving some thought to the charity fund-raiser Kim was helping him plan. He didn't know why it hadn't occurred to him earlier. He wanted her to do more than help him plan the event.

He kissed her tenderly on the lips savoring the taste that he found so addictive. "I have something to ask you."

"Okay." Her heart pounded wildly. She didn't know what to expect. Was he about to say what she wanted to hear?

"It's about the fund-raiser…" He placed another kiss on her lips as he tried to gather the proper words.

She furrowed her brow in a moment's confusion accompanied by a hint of disappointment. "The charity event? Is there a problem of some sort?"

"Not at all. I was wondering if you'd, uh, if you'd act as my hostess for the event. I know school will be in session then and you'll be teaching, but the fund-raiser will be in San Francisco, and I think we should plan it for a Saturday night.''

His question came as a complete surprise. It was not at all what she had anticipated. Had she heard him correctly? ''You mean you want me to attend the event? To be your date?''

''More than just a date. I want you to help me greet the guests, socialize with them and in general help me make sure everyone has a good time. I want you to be my partner in hosting the event, to be intricately involved in everything that's going on. I want you to be much more involved and visible than someone behind the scenes planning what others will enjoy. I want you to be able to take credit for your contribution to its success.''

The words rang in her ears—*be my partner…take credit for your contribution*. It was a very gracious gesture, one that showed his willingness to allow other people to share the spotlight rather than needing to be the center of attention himself. It was the same way he used his nonprofit organization to do good things where he didn't want his name detracting from the meaning of the project.

''I would be honored.'' Her spirits soared on the wings of his words, and delight filled her heart. He hadn't told her he loved her or offered her any commitment, but perhaps this was the most he was capable of. It was enough for her to know he cared for her very much even if he didn't say the words she wanted to hear. She basked in the glow of what he had said and the implications of the words he had uttered with such sincerity.

It was several minutes before Kim finally made an effort to disengage herself from his embrace. ''Chloe should be awake by now. She'll need to get up.''

He held her tighter, stopping her from getting out of bed.

"Hmm…I know you're right, but this feels so good that I hate to move."

"I need to check on Chloe."

"I don't hear any noise coming from her room. If she's awake she's apparently content where she is." He cupped her breast, caressing the gentle curve and teasing her nipple. "And I know I'm certainly content with where I am. Are you sure I can't tempt you to stay here for a little bit longer?"

"Well…" She succumbed to his touch and the excitement it created, melting into his arms once again.

"Doggy…doggy?" The little voice came from the guest room, putting a stop to the enticing seduction he had initiated.

Kim sat upright, her gaze darting toward the bedroom door. "We'd better check on her."

Jared heaved a sigh of resignation. "You're right." He finally turned her loose, climbed out of bed and placed a soft kiss on her forehead. "Stay here. I'll be right back." He went straight to his dresser. A moment later he returned to the bed with a large football jersey and a bathrobe. He held them both toward her. "Are you sure there isn't enough time to take a shower first?" The twinkle in his eyes matched his mischievous grin. "You could soap my back and I'd soap your front and then we could…" His voice trailed off, but there was no mistaking his intention.

"That's a very tempting offer, but I don't think now is the right time to pursue it."

"Unfortunately, you're right. Instead, I'll give you a choice of what you'd like to throw on before venturing across the hall."

She looked at the two proffered garments, then at Jared. She couldn't stop the grin that tugged at the corners of her mouth.

He sat next to her. "Never let it be said that I don't learn from my mistakes."

She grabbed the football jersey and slipped it over her head. When she stood, the hem came halfway to her knees. She leaned forward and placed a quick kiss on his lips. "This will do for the moment."

She hurried across the hall. Chloe was trying to climb out of the crib. Kim lifted the little girl out of the bed, kissed her on the cheek and gave her a big smile. "Good morning, Chloe. It looks like I got here just in time to keep you from hurting yourself."

She quickly tended to the toddler's needs, then they went to the kitchen where Jared had just finished making coffee after pulling on a pair of sweatpants. He took a couple of mugs from the cupboard and set them on the counter. He turned his attention to Chloe, picking up the little girl and giving her a hug and kiss on the cheek.

"Good morning, Chloe. Are you ready for breakfast?"

The toddler squirmed in his arms and she looked around the kitchen. "Doggy? Doggy?"

Jared chuckled as he put her on the floor. He glanced at Kim. "She and Lurch have formed quite an attachment for each other."

"That's good. Lurch will be good protection for her if…" How strange fate was. She had forgotten that Chloe was only a temporary resident in Jared's house, that his attorney was searching for her mother. For a moment it had seemed as if they were a family. She had liked the feeling, liked it very much. But was it more than was possible for her to have?

"I'll fix breakfast if you want to grab a shower and get dressed. And I'm not suggesting in any way that you should leave. It's just that we're obviously not going to be able to finish what we started…'' He gave her a brief, loving kiss. ''At least not right now.''

He cocked his head and looked at her questioningly. His green eyes sparkled with seduction and passion. ''Perhaps we could retire for a little nap at the same time as Chloe and pick up where we left off?''

Ten

The next week was a busy one for Kim. The excitement surrounding the charity project energized her. But even more, she thrived on the time she and Jared had together, such as the stolen hours when Chloe took her naps. What had started as a grudging barter arrangement to exchange work hours for her father's debt had become the center of her life. Being at Jared's house every day and sharing the care of the toddler had almost taken on the feel of a family…the warmth, caring, giving and love. It all felt so very right.

But she stopped short of moving into his house. He had suggested she bring some clothes so she could stay overnight on those occasions when they *worked late,* but she had refused his offer. Without a commitment to a relationship she didn't want to put herself in a position when it would be even more difficult and heartbreaking if something should happen between them—if Jared should become tired of the arrangement.

Each night she returned to her father's house. The real estate agent had a couple who were interested in the property and were going to make an offer. Kim wanted to be ready to vacate the house as soon as it sold. She worked on packing the items she would be sending to her place in San Francisco and sorting out what would stay with the house and what remaining items she would need to dispose of. She finally found some time to go through the last of the boxes of her father's belongings, including the box where she had placed the file folders.

She looked through the first folder. The papers seemed to be endless lists of things such as tours he wanted to take in various places around the United States, foreign countries and cities he wanted to visit, books he wanted to read, movies he wanted to see, remodeling he wanted to do to the house, people from his past he wanted to call and hobbies he wanted to pursue. The one thing the lists seemed to have in common was the fact that they were all things left undone. A wave of sadness washed over her. Had he started making the lists after he found out about his heart condition? Her sigh of resignation escaped into the quiet of the house. She would never know. She set the folder aside.

The next folder contained personal correspondence between her father and his brother, who had died ten years earlier. She glanced at the letters and skimmed through a couple of them. They didn't seem to contain anything pertinent to her or to his estate. She set that aside, too.

She picked up two more folders, but like the one filled with the personal letters, they didn't have any relevance to his estate. She picked up the last folder.

The name of Ron Stevens jumped out at her. She carefully examined each piece of paper. The file contained a meticulous listing of each contact between her father and Ron Stevens and between her father and various employees of Stevens Enterprises, notations of both phone conversations and written material. She spread the papers out on the dining room table.

After two hours of carefully going over each piece of paper in the folder she leaned back in her chair, drained and exhausted. She didn't know what to think. She could feel her father's anger and bitterness in his handwritten notes, which comprised her father's case for why he didn't owe the twenty thousand dollars to Stevens Enterprises in spite of the signed documents Jared had shown her.

Her father had made some valid comments about extenuating circumstances surrounding the business transaction—circumstances that occurred after he had signed the contract and promissory note. It seemed to her as though the incidents he mentioned should have rendered the debt invalid.

She tried to put everything in a logical, unbiased perspective. Why had her father allowed the conflict over the debt to go on for so many years? Nowhere in the file had she found any papers relating to her father's attorney, only the attorney for Stevens Enterprises. If her father's position was legitimate, why hadn't he consulted an attorney about the matter?

Was Jared aware of the circumstances? None of the notations included his name. A sinking feeling settled in the pit of her stomach. As much as she didn't want Jared to have any involvement, she could not dismiss the possibility. She returned the papers to the file folder and set it next to her purse. She would talk to Jared about it in the morning and get his perspective on the information. After all, that's what he told her he wanted her to do if she had any questions or problems with anything he had said or done. Well, this was definitely a problem.

Kim finally called it a night and went to bed. The information in the file folder continued to swirl inside her head, leaving her uneasy. The path she had traveled over the past few weeks that led to Jared's bed and her silent acknowledgment of her love had started from a totally improbable place, and she had moved along it at lightning speed, but the trip was not without its share of tension accompanied by several ups and downs.

She had thought all that was behind her, that they had worked their way through the obstacles and put the generations-old family feud to rest. But the conflict that had thrown them together had reared its head again. The twenty-thousand-dollar debt—was it legitimate or one of the many dark moments between the Stevens and Donaldson families? This time, however, she had learned her lesson. She would not make any assumptions, nor would she dwell on what might or might not be. She would go to Jared with her father's notes and ask him for an explanation. A dark cloud of trepidation began to descend over her. She fought to keep it away. Jared would be able to explain everything. Surely he would be able to explain.

Her eyes grew heavy until she was finally asleep. When she woke the next morning she quickly prepared for another day at work. She arrived at Jared's house early to help get Chloe up, dressed and fed.

Jared let her in, pausing long enough to place a loving kiss on her lips. "Come on, we're in the kitchen having breakfast. I saved some for you."

To her surprise, Kim found that Jared had already taken care of Chloe's needs and was just finishing with the toddler's breakfast. An amused chuckle escaped her throat as she watched him wipe the sticky syrup from the little girl's hands and face.

"I seem to have arrived a little late, but it appears that you have things well in hand. What time did she wake up?"

"About an hour ago. I wasn't ready to get up yet, but duty called and put an end to that extra hour of sleep I wanted."

She extended a knowing smile toward Jared. "That's the way it is when you have a toddler in the house. Your time and your life are no longer your own."

He slipped his arms around her, pulling her body against his. He brushed a soft kiss against her lips, nibbled at the corners of her mouth, then brought his mouth down fully on hers. It was the type of kiss that curled her toes and made her body tingle, the type of kiss that would have ended in his bed had it not been for Chloe's presence.

He broke off the kiss, his voice carrying the same reluctance to let go as she felt. "I definitely have noticed that certain things need to be more carefully coordinated these days."

Kim stepped away from his very disarming touch. The charity event was coming together nicely, but there was still a lot of work to be done. She thought about the file folder with her father's notes. She needed to find some time to talk to Jared about that, but not now, not with Chloe being the center of attention for the moment. The discussion could wait until later that day when a more businesslike atmosphere surrounded them, and they wouldn't be interrupted.

A nervous twinge pushed at her as if something deep inside was trying to tell her to stay away from a discussion of her father's notes—to let the controversy die its natural death. She shoved the feeling away. She needed the answers so she could tie up the loose ends and answer the questions the notes had presented to her, things she thought she'd already put to rest until she read her father's notes.

It was a new dimension added to the ongoing conflict still pushing inside her about her relationship with Jared, a conflict she had not been able to forget regardless of how much she wanted to ignore it. Where were they headed? What type of relationship did they have? The questions continued to nag at her, the only negatives in what had turned out to be a surprisingly wonderful summer, made so by the man she had fallen hopelessly in love with and the laughter of an innocent little girl in need of a stable home.

Kim reached out and took Chloe's hand. "Come on. Let's see what's in your playroom, and then I need to get to work." They walked from the kitchen to the converted conference room. As soon as she got the toddler settled, she turned to the invitation list for the charity event. They had settled on a date, and she had confirmed the hotel ballroom. Next came the printing of the invitations.

After combining the two lists and eliminating the duplicates, four hundred invitations needed to be addressed and mailed. She ordered five hundred invitations from the printer, which would be available in two weeks. Things were starting to come together nicely, although there was still a lot of work to do. She stopped periodically to relive the thrill that rushed through her when Jared had asked her to be his hostess and attend the fund-raiser with him. They had been working on the event as a team and now they would attend it the same way.

The morning passed quickly. To her surprise Jared took charge of Chloe's midmorning snack and put her down for a short nap. It warmed her heart to see the way he doted on the little girl. A slight frown wrinkled her brow. What would happen when his attorney found Chloe's mother? The little girl had already been at his house far longer than either of them thought would be the case. It had started to feel normal and natural to have her as part of the household. Chloe seemed happy and content, and she was being well cared for by Jared, Fred, Kim and Lurch. But would the child welfare people consider it a proper home environment?

As if her concerns had been a portent of things to come, Jared's attorney called after lunch. She could tell from the hushed tones coming from Jared's office that it was not a good conversation. A few minutes later he appeared next to her desk. His somber expression said it all.

"That—" he gestured toward his office "—was about Chloe. The detective found her mother. Grant is driving to Oakland to see her."

"What happens next?"

"We'll know more this evening when he gets back. He said he'd come right here after his meeting with her."

"I suppose the next step is to finally call the authorities...." Her voice trailed off when she saw the defiance flash across his face. She reached out and lightly touched his arm. "Jared, you've known all along that eventually the police would have to be notified about her being abandoned by both her mother and father."

He took her hand in his. His voice was soft, his words filled with sorrow. "I know."

Jared pulled Kim out of the chair and into his arms. He held her in his embrace, reveling in the closeness and warmth she brought to him. The last few weeks had been the best of his entire life. He was the happiest he had ever been, with Kim as an all important part of his life and Chloe to fill out the family. It had been the sense of family he had been searching for all his adult life, which had managed to elude him until now.

Kim felt the tension in Jared's body, and it added to the

stress that had been building inside her over the past couple of hours. She had to confront him about her father's notes, about the extenuating circumstances surrounding the twenty-thousand-dollar debt. But was now the appropriate time?

Was there any such thing as an appropriate time?

Once again she entertained the thought of forgetting about it, but finally dismissed that possibility from her mind. Jared had made her promise she would tell him when something was wrong, when he had said or done anything that upset her. She had to know the truth in order to find closure with the entire business of the debt and the larger scope of the generations-old feud between Jared's family and her own.

She didn't know what the future held for the two of them. Regardless of what she wanted, the fact remained that he had never said he loved her, nor had he offered her any commitment. She couldn't be sure they had a permanent future together, but until she resolved yesterday's issues she couldn't successfully plan for tomorrow. The question would always be in the back of her mind trying to force its way between them.

Perhaps now would be the best time, while Chloe was taking her nap. They could put this matter behind them before Grant Collins returned from seeing Chloe's mother. Then they could tackle the next issue without any encumbrances.

"Jared?" Kim nervously cleared her throat. "Uh…"

He looked at her quizzically, his brow wrinkled in a slight frown. "What's wrong?"

She took a steadying breath, then plunged into what was on her mind. "I came across something last night that bothers me. I was going through some of my father's files, things I had put aside after he died and am just now getting to. There was one file—" she glanced away, not sure she wanted to face the possibilities she was opening "—uh, it contained detailed notes about his ongoing confrontation with your father and with other members of your company over the twenty-thousand-dollar debt. He's listed several…irregularities that he uncovered."

"Irregularities?"

"Yes, information about wrongdoing on your father's part, promises made but never delivered, a whole list of underhanded and possibly even illegal events that surrounded the contract…things that should have rendered the debt null and void."

She handed him a neatly typed list she had put together showing a chronological chain of events and her father's allegations. Many of the points of contention happened after the signing of the contract and promissory note.

He took the piece of paper from her without comment. She watched his expression as he studied the list. He didn't say anything as he glanced at the floor, then out the window. He didn't need to say anything. The expression on his face was not one of confusion, surprise or shock. It said she had not provided him with anything he hadn't already known. The moment she had feared, the moment that had gnawed at her insides was now reality.

"Jared?" She tried to keep the hurt and growing anger out of her voice. She didn't want to make the mistake of jumping to conclusions, as she had in the past. "Please talk to me. Tell me this isn't what I think. Explain what it means." The desperation to have it not be what she feared filled her with dread and anxiety. "Say something, please…anything."

"I don't have a ready explanation. I suspected that there was something amiss about the deal, but I didn't have any proof."

Her eyes grew wide at the realization of his words. "You

suspected? You thought there had been underhanded deal-ings by your father, yet you never mentioned it to me?" She couldn't hide her hurt other than to mask it with her anger. "You allowed me to continue working off my fa-ther's alleged debt as if I were some kind of an indentured servant?"

"Indentured servant? That's not a very fair statement."

Her voice rose as her anger came pouring out. "Not a very fair statement? Do you think it was *fair* of you to manipulate me into working for you to satisfy a debt that you freely admit you had some reservations about?"

His voice rose to match hers. "I didn't think it was unfair in light of what your father had done to mine."

"What my father did? What are you talking about?"

"I'm talking about all the shoddy merchandise your fa-ther sold mine, merchandise my father paid for in good faith before he had inspected it. Your father certainly never refunded my father's money for that sneaky little deal."

"If that's so, then why didn't your attorney make an issue of that rather than the promissory note?"

Jared didn't answer her. He didn't have an answer. He hadn't wanted to deal with the whole can of worms that had been the many small business dealings between Ron Stevens and Paul Donaldson. It was almost as if it were a game being played by two bitter men to see which one could cause the most trouble for the other. *You cheated me in the last deal, now it's my turn to cheat you.*

It was a game he hadn't wanted to get suckered into. The contract and promissory note had been different. They were tangible business documents detailing a transaction that had already been run through the corporate accounting offices.

Kim had wanted an answer—one that wouldn't break her heart. She hadn't gotten it. Sorrow filled her words. "I guess your silence says it all. Your previous words about ending the feud and putting the sins of past generations behind us were nothing more than empty words.''

She removed her purse from the desk drawer. With trembling fingers she withdrew her car keys, then took a calming breath and walked toward the door. She paused for a moment and turned toward him.

Her icy words cut through the stilled air. ''I consider the matter of the alleged debt satisfied. I'll be returning to my apartment in San Francisco in the morning.'' A well of emotion shoved out her final words as a sob caught in her throat. ''When Chloe wakes up from her nap, tell her goodbye for me…tell her I love her very much.'' With that, Kim turned and ran out the door.

Jared remained riveted to the spot, unable to move or speak and barely able to think. A moment later he heard her car drive away. A sick churning in the pit of his stomach spurred him into action. He charged out the door, but was too late. He saw her car disappear down the driveway and turn into the street. He could catch her if he hurried. He dashed inside, grabbed a set of keys from his desk and headed for the door.

A scream followed by the loud cries of a small child brought him to an abrupt halt. *Chloe.* In his desperate need to stop Kim he had completely forgotten about Chloe. He felt as if he were being torn in two directions. Half of him wanted to go after Kim and the other half knew he couldn't leave Chloe alone. The immediacy of the toddler's cries made his decision for him. He hurried toward her bedroom.

He had been treading in unknown territory from the moment he met Kim, and now he was so far removed from anything he knew or understood he didn't know where to begin. The woman he loved, the woman he wanted to spend the rest of his life with, had just walked out his door after announcing she was leaving town, and he had done nothing to stop her. He had never even worked up the courage to tell her he loved her.

He entered Chloe's bedroom and immediately discovered the problem. The toddler stood in the crib trying to climb out. Her teddy bear rested on the floor next to the bed. A moment later Lurch came running into the room. The large dog brushed past Jared, picked up the teddy bear in his mouth and carried it over to the crib so the little girl could reach it.

Jared picked her up from the crib and carried her toward the kitchen. "Are you ready for some lunch?" He may have been paying attention to Chloe, but his thoughts were on Kim and what he needed to do to get her back. She would be leaving Otter Crest in the morning. He had to come up with something before then.

Eleven

Kim stared at herself in the bathroom mirror. The red, puffy eyes that said she had been crying stared at her. She had never felt as devastated in her life as she did at that moment. To say she was heartbroken would be a colossal understatement. Everything had gotten out of hand with anger and recriminations on both sides. Her entire life had become a complete shambles, and she was an emotional wreck.

Had she done the right thing in leaving? What else could she have done? A relationship couldn't be built on deceit, and holding back information was the same as lying. Jared suspected his father had cheated her father, which made the debt invalid, yet he had never said anything. She shook her head as she tried to sort out what was real. He had never offered her any commitment. Did they even *have* a relationship? She was so confused…and so miserable.

And Chloe—the toddler who was only supposed to be

at Jared's house for a day or so—had also become a part of her life. It felt like a real family when the three of them were together. It was a feeling she had grown to cherish. And now it was gone, too.

She looked around at the boxes she had packed. More than closing a chapter of her life, she was closing two chapters. One chapter dealt with her sometimes strained and occasionally turbulent relationship with her father and the other chapter with the man she loved with all her heart…a love that would never be returned. A heavy dose of sorrow shuddered through her body. Somehow she would get on with her life, but she wasn't sure exactly how.

She forced herself back to her packing. She would take as much with her in her car as she could and get the rest in a few days when she could borrow a van from a friend.

The ringing phone broke the silence. As soon as she answered it she heard Jared's panicked voice.

"Chloe has disappeared. I can't find her anywhere. I need your help. Hurry."

There was no mistaking the urgency in his voice. It wasn't a ploy of some sort, another bit of deceit. If the little girl had gotten outside, she could have wandered off anywhere, including down to the beach or out on the boat dock. A sinking feeling crashed inside her. Chloe could have…

Kim stopped her wild, scattered thoughts. Chloe was all right. She had to be. Kim refused to allow any other possibility. A rush of adrenaline pushed her into action. She grabbed her car keys and darted out the door.

A few minutes later she pulled up in front of Jared's house. He stood at the open front door, the expression on his face saying he had been anxiously waiting for her. She jumped out of her car and ran up the steps to the porch.

"Have you found her yet? What happened?"

Jared pulled her into his arms and hugged her tightly

against his body. He wanted to say so many things to her. Primary among them was that he loved her and didn't want to lose her. But as important as that was, finding Chloe took priority. His movements were as frantic as his words. "I'm so glad you're here. I've looked everywhere. I don't know how she got away. One minute she was in the kitchen, and when I turned around, she was gone." He released her from his embrace but continued to hold on to her hand. "I thought I had a watchful eye on her. I thought I…" His words trailed off as the despair covered his face.

"Don't blame yourself."

His emotionally frantic state came out in his voice. "Don't blame myself? How can I not blame myself? I was the one responsible for her. I was the one who insisted on keeping her here when you wanted to call the police. If something has happened to her, who else's fault could it possibly be? The blame is solely mine."

They walked inside the house and he closed the front door. Kim's gaze darted from place to place. "You've searched everywhere inside the house? In closets? Under beds? Behind the floor-length drapes? You've checked low cupboards even though they seemed to be fastened shut? Did you look in the basement? In the garage?"

"Yes, I've done all of those things. She just isn't here."

A sick churning worked its way up her throat. "Could someone have taken her? Maybe her mother coming for her? Or Terry changing his mind?"

"No. Grant is seeing the mother right now, and he never told her where Chloe was. And as for Terry…well, I can't imagine him doing anything that would create even the slightest bit of inconvenience for himself. You do remember how quickly he dumped her off on me, don't you?"

Kim took in a steadying breath in an attempt to calm her rampaging fears. She could see how genuinely distraught

Jared was. She needed to keep her cool and handle this logically in spite of the fact that her emotions were completely involved. It wouldn't do for both of them to not be thinking clearly, although he did seem to have done a very thorough search of the house. She steeled herself against the emotional onslaught that threatened to overwhelm her.

"Have you searched the grounds yet? You've got two acres here with lots of plants and shrubbery."

"No, I haven't looked outside yet."

"Toddlers can disappear in the blink of an eye and hide in very small spaces."

They started with the heavily landscaped front yard, checking behind and in all the bushes and flower beds. Then they moved to the backyard.

They stood on the deck looking across the yard. Kim's gaze fell on the swimming pool and hot tub. A hard jolt of trepidation shot through her body. The panic she had been trying to keep under control refused to stay submerged.

"Jared...I know you have the cover on the pool and hot tub, but could she have somehow crawled under—"

"No. That was the first thing I checked. But I'll look again."

He lifted the heavy lid from the hot tub so Kim could look inside, then replaced it. Next he flipped the switch that retracted the automatic pool cover. They both watched as more and more of the water came into view. When the pool was fully uncovered and Kim was satisfied, he reversed the process, and they watched until the pool was once again completely covered.

The anxiety continued to run rampant through her as they started a careful search of the backyard. With each passing minute Kim became more anxious and scared. She glanced at Jared. She could tell from the expression on his face that he was every bit as worried as she was, yet he managed to project an outer calm that gave her confidence everything would be all right. It somehow eased the full-blown panic that had gripped her from the moment of his phone call.

Lurch lay in front of his doghouse watching them as if he was wondering what in the world they could be doing. Jared searched through the shrubbery along the sidewall enclosing the backyard while Kim did the same on the opposite wall. They worked their way to the back of the property. Jared checked the lock on the back gate leading to the stairs that went down to the beach and the boat dock.

"The lock is secure. There's no way she could have gotten out of the yard through the gate, and she certainly couldn't have climbed over an eight-foot wall."

Jared took Kim's hand in his. He desperately needed the warmth of the physical contact. He loved her so very much. Through his stupidity and fears he had managed to drive her away. It felt as if his entire world had collapsed around him. Then, when he thought things could not possibly be worse, Chloe had disappeared. Somehow he had to bring the three of them back together again. Kim was there, and now they had to find Chloe.

A new thought hit him. His head snapped around toward her, and his eyes grew wide. His words came out excited and urgent. "The deck...I never looked under the deck."

They raced across the yard toward the house. Jared went into the utility room and returned a minute later with a large flashlight. He pulled open the access panel covering the entrance to the area beneath the large wooden deck.

"I don't think she could have pulled off this panel and I can't imagine how she could have put it back in place from under the deck, but I've got to check it out anyway." He got down on his stomach and, using his arms, he pulled himself through the opening.

He switched on the flashlight, shined the bright beam

around the darkened area and carefully searched every foot of space. He pulled himself over to the place where the hot tub had been set into the deck and carefully checked all the way around the tub base. When he was satisfied that Chloe wasn't there, he crawled out from under the deck and replaced the access door.

Kim's anxious words greeted him. "Well?"

His voice carried the disappointment that coursed through him. "She's not there." He tried to brush some of the dirt from the front of his clothes. Despair surrounded his words. "I don't know where else to look."

He took her hand and led her inside the house. He paused at the door leading from the utility room to the kitchen. He couldn't hide the turmoil churning inside him. "I can't think of anything else to do or anyplace else to look. Can you?"

"You've already searched the inside of the house thoroughly, and we've covered all of the outside." She blinked several times in an effort to brush away the tears gathering in her eyes. She tried to swallow the lump forming in her throat, but it came out as a sob. "I don't know what else to suggest."

He brought her hand to his mouth and kissed her palm. He had never felt so helpless. "I guess it's time to call the police."

Lurch pushed his way through his doggy door into the utility room. He let out a bark, then sat down and stared at them as if trying to convey some message.

Kim kneeled next to the Saint Bernard. She gave his head a loving stroke. "What's the matter, Lurch? Do you miss Chloe, too?"

At the mention of the toddler's name Lurch jumped up and barked a couple of times, then went out the doggy door. He barked again from outside the house.

Kim's gaze flew to Jared, and she saw a look of recognition that matched the sudden realization that had hit her. "Do you suppose Lurch is trying to tell us where Chloe is?"

They rushed out the door. Lurch barked again, then trotted over to his doghouse, pausing along the way to look at them as if making sure they were following.

A tingle of excitement started deep inside Kim and quickly spread through her body. Jared still held her hand. A moment later he gave it a reassuring squeeze along with a confident smile, telling her everything was all right.

He got down on his hands and knees and peeked into the doghouse. It wasn't until he expelled the air from his lungs that he realized he had been holding his breath in anticipation of what he hoped to find. A wave of relief washed over him. Chloe had curled up on Lurch's blanket and was sound asleep.

He reached inside the doghouse and brought out the sleeping toddler. He carried her to Kim, his words soft and soothing as he walked even though the sleeping child couldn't hear them. "You gave us quite a scare, Chloe. We didn't know where you'd gone and we were very worried."

Kim could not stop the big smile from spreading across her face. The exhilaration welled inside her and pushed out in the form of a soft laugh. "I was scared to death."

"She must have crawled out through Lurch's dog door, maybe following him when he went outside. She's still sleeping."

"She's probably exhausted from her big adventure."

He looked questioningly at Kim. "Is it all right if we put her in her crib and worry about giving her a bath later?"

"Of course."

Jared and Kim walked through the house to Chloe's bedroom, the child securely nestled in his arms. He placed her lovingly in the crib. They stood and watched her for a few minutes. Jared put his arm around Kim's shoulder and drew her close to him.

His words were soft and heartfelt. "What started as my being responsible for her has grown into so much more. It's as if she's part of my life, and to have to give her up to the child welfare people will be like losing a piece of me."

He pulled Kim into his arms. His soft words tickled across her cheek. "And losing you would be like losing all of me."

He placed a loving kiss on her lips, then held her face in his hands. He looked deeply into her eyes. "I don't care about the debt. I don't care about the feud. I don't care about whose father did what. All I care about is the two of us being together."

Jared took a calming breath to steady his rattled nerves, then finally managed to say what he had been holding in his heart.

"I love you, Kim. I love you very much. I didn't mean to hurt you. Please forgive me."

She placed her hands on top of his. She felt the trembling, but didn't know if it was Jared or herself. Had she heard him correctly? Could he have said what she had been longing to hear? Her words came out as a breathless whisper. "You're not saying that just because you think it's what I want to hear, are you?"

"No. I'm saying it because I'm not afraid to say it anymore. I love you, Kim. I've been so afraid of the emotion and scared to death of the commitment that goes with it, but watching you walk out of my life this afternoon frightened me even more."

Her unbridled joy erupted full force. She flung her arms around his neck. "I love you, too. I really do. I love you."

He captured her mouth with all the love that had been inside him wanting to get out. His tongue meshed with hers. He twined his fingers in her hair, caressed her shoulders and snuggled her hips tightly against his. Where the passion between them had always been hot and electric, now the final missing piece was in place to complete the picture, and that piece was love…deep and abiding love.

Jared broke off the kiss but continued to hold her in his arms.

"I've got dirt all over me from crawling around under the deck and I've probably gotten some on you, too. I need to take a shower." He flashed a sexy inviting smile. "Perhaps we could take a shower together?"

She nestled her head against his shoulder as the sweetness of the moment swirled inside her. The total impact of the last several minutes, of Jared's declaration of love, still had her senses somewhat numbed. It was what she had wanted more than anything, and now that it was a reality she was having difficulty taking it all in. "That sounds like a fun idea, but I don't have any other clothes to put on. Besides, isn't your attorney due here sometime soon?"

He rested his cheek against the top of her head. "You're right. Grant is probably on his way now."

Jared released her from his embrace as he looked at his clothes. "I really do need to take a quick shower and put on something clean."

"You go ahead and grab a shower. Meanwhile, I have plenty of work to do in the office."

Jared placed a loving kiss on her lips, then disappeared across the hall to his bedroom. After checking on Chloe to make sure she was still sleeping, Kim went to the office. She picked up where she had left the charity event. About twenty minutes later she looked up to find Jared staring at her.

"I didn't hear you come in."

He walked over to her and sat on the edge of the desk. "You looked like you were deep in concentration. I didn't want to disturb you. What you are—"

The doorbell interrupted him.

"I'll bet that's Grant." He hurried to the door and admitted his attorney to the house. He called down the hall for Kim to join them in the den.

Grant Collins nodded in Kim's direction, acknowledging her presence. "Miss Donaldson. It's nice to see you again."

A flush of embarrassment heated her cheeks. "I want to apologize for my rude behavior. There was no excuse for what I did."

"That's quite all right. I understand." The attorney went right to the business at hand.

"I've spoken with Amy Fenton, the little girl's mother. She does not want the child back. At first she told me it was because there was no way she could properly care for her, but her true reasons came to light shortly after that. It seems she has a new boyfriend who has no interest in being saddled with the care of any children. He wants to be free to pursue his wanderings and expects Amy to go with him. She had made the choice between Chloe and the new boyfriend—she chose the boyfriend."

Jared's frown carried a hint of confusion and a lot of disgust at the news his attorney had brought him. "So what happens now? Where does Chloe go?"

Grant drew in a deep breath and slowly expelled it. "Well, a lot of that hinges on Terry. He is Chloe's father and apparently is listed as such on the birth certificate."

"Terry? He'll never take any responsibility for raising a child. He certainly demonstrated that by bringing Chloe here, then announcing that he was leaving on an extended vacation starting immediately."

Kim had been following the discussion with great interest. "If Terry doesn't want her, what will happen? Will she become a ward of the state and be put into an orphanage?"

A look of deep concern covered Grant's face. "I'm afraid that's probably how it will happen."

Jared looked at Kim, his eyes pleading as much as his voice. "Let's adopt her…you and me."

"What?" The shock quickly filled every corner of her conscious thoughts. His statement had come out of the clear blue, and she wasn't sure what to say.

Jared pulled her into his arms. "Marry me. We'll adopt Chloe. We'll be a real family."

"Do you realize what you're saying?" She was afraid to allow her joy to burst into the open, afraid he didn't understand the full impact of what he had said.

"Yes, I know exactly what I'm saying. I love you. I want you to marry me. I want us to adopt Chloe."

She threw her arms around his neck as the tears of joy ran down her cheeks. Her happiness welled inside her until there was hardly any room left for her to breathe. "Yes, yes, yes! I'll marry you!"

He placed a loving kiss on her lips. "I'm now the luckiest man in the world. I have everything I want, everything that's important…a wife and a daughter to love forever. For the first time in my life I have a real family."

"Uh…" Grant cleared his throat, but when he didn't receive a response he made his way toward the front door. "I'll call you in the morning."

A moment later the sound of the front door opening and closing filled the room.

Jared held Kim tightly in his embrace. A mischievous grin tugged at the corners of his mouth. "I was beginning to think he'd never leave."

She returned his teasing smile. "Me, too."

"Kimbra Stevens...Mrs. Kimbra Stevens...Mrs. Jared Stevens... I hope you like the sound of those names because they'll belong to you just as soon as we can make it legal."

"I love the sound of those names. I love *you*."

Jared continued to hold her in his embrace. The warmth and contentment radiated between them and spoke of a deep and lasting love.

Epilogue

Kim and Jared stood next to the crib watching Chloe as she slept. He turned to Kim, placed a loving kiss on her lips, then folded her into his embrace.

"Tell me, Mrs. Stevens, is all of this real? I keep asking myself if it's possible to have everything I want and to be as deliriously happy as I am, yet here it all is—a wife I love very much and a darling little daughter to make us a family."

She rested her head against his shoulder. "I know what you mean. Everything happened so quickly, it's taking me a while to catch up with reality."

"I thought it would take longer for all the paperwork on Chloe. Grant really earned his money on this one. He had the appropriate documents drawn up in record time, got the mother's signature and Terry's signature showing that they relinquished all claim to the child and gave her up for adoption."

Kim reached over and adjusted Chloe's blanket, then they walked quietly out of Chloe's bedroom and continued outside to the deck. The full moon cast a silvery glow over everything, enveloping them in a mystical aura.

"I love you, Jared. I really do."

He let out a soft chuckle. "It's a good thing, Mrs. Stevens, because you're stuck with me forever."

"I like the sound of that...Mrs. Stevens forever."

Jared pulled her into his arms. She wrapped her arms around his waist and nestled her head against his shoulder. It was, indeed, a love that would last forever.

*   *   *   *   *

#1495 AMBER BY NIGHT—Sharon Sala

Amelia Beauchamp needed money, so she transformed herself from a plain-Jane librarian into a seductive siren named Amber and took a second job as a cocktail waitress. Then in walked irresistible Tyler Savage. The former Casanova wanted her as much as she wanted him, but Amelia was playing a dangerous game. Would Tyler still want her once he discovered her true identity?

#1496 SLEEPING WITH HER RIVAL—Sheri WhiteFeather

Dynasties: The Barones

After a sabotage incident left her family's company with a public-relations nightmare, Gina Barone was forced to work with hotshot PR consultant Flint Kingman. Flint decided a very public pretend affair was the perfect distraction. But the passion that exploded between Gina and heartbreakingly handsome Flint was all too real, and she found herself yearning to make their temporary arrangement last forever.

#1497 RENEGADE MILLIONAIRE—Kristi Gold

When sexy Dr. Rio Madrid learned lovely Joanna Blake was living in a slum, he did the gentlemanly thing and asked her to move in with him. But his feelings for her proved to be anything but gentlemanly—he wanted to kiss her senseless! However, Joanna wouldn't accept less than his whole heart, and he didn't know if he could give her that.

#1498 MAIL-ORDER PRINCE IN HER BED—Kathryn Jensen

Because of an office prank, shy Maria McPherson found herself being whisked away in a limousine by Antonio Boniface. But Antonio was not just any mail-order escort. He was a real prince—and when virginal Maria asked him to tutor her in the ways of love, Antonio eagerly agreed. But Maria yearned for a life with Antonio. Could she convince him to risk everything for love?

#1499 THE COWBOY CLAIMS HIS LADY—Meagan McKinney

Matched in Montana

Rancher Bruce Everett had sworn off women for good, so he was fit to be tied when stressed-out city girl Melynda Cray came to his ranch for a little rest and relaxation. Still, Melynda had a way about her that got under the stubborn cowboy's skin, and soon he was courting his lovely guest. But Melynda had been hurt before; could Bruce prove his love was rock solid?

#1500 TANGLED SHEETS, TANGLED LIES—Julie Hogan

Cole Travis vowed to find the son he hadn't known he had. His sleuthing led him to Jem—and Jem's adoptive mother, beguiling beauty Lauren Simpson. In order to find out for sure if the boy was his son, Cole posed as a handyman and offered his services to Lauren. But as Cole fell under Lauren's captivating spell…he just hoped their love would survive the truth.

SDCNM0203